I Don't Want To Be Like Her

by Marcia Kruchten

Cover photo by
The Photographic Illustrators

Published by Willowisp Press, Inc.
401 E. Wilson Bridge Road, Worthington, Ohio 43085

Printed in the United States of America

10 9 8 7 6 5 4 3 2 1

ISBN 0-87406-064-8

For my mother,
Helen Bonner Chambers

One

IT was a perfect fall Sunday, crisp and clear. Shelley Carter slid into the backseat of the family car. Most of the crowd had already left the parking lot after church. But Shelley's parents were still on the steps chatting with friends.

While Shelley waited for her mom and dad she was admiring the colorful trees that sheltered the church. She noticed how the red and yellow leaves seemed to frame the familiar white building against the bright blue October sky.

"It looks like a painting," Shelley said to herself, contented.

"It's pretty," a voice agreed.

Shelley jumped, startled. Cindy Brooks stuck her smiling face through the open car window.

"When did you start talking to yourself?"

Cindy asked as she opened the door.

"Just since I turned fourteen," Shelley said, straight-faced. "That's when my brain turned to mush. Why are you getting into my car?"

Cindy plopped down on the seat beside Shelley. "Because I'm going home with you, that's why. Your mom told my mom I could come to your house for dinner. My folks will pick me up later. They have to go somewhere. What are you having for dinner, anyway?"

"Oh, something's in the oven. . . a roast, I guess. Where's your brother, Jimmy?" Shelley asked, looking out the window. "Is he coming, too?"

"Nope," Cindy replied. "He's at Grandma's."

"You mean, we can actually talk to each other without. . ."

"Without the brat," Cindy finished smugly.

"No kidding," Shelley cried. "Hey, we can paint our nails."

"Or we can walk downtown after dinner," Cindy suggested, wiggling her eyebrows wildly. "Alone!"

Shelley laughed. Cindy was always fun to be with. Shelley remembered when her older sister, Jackie, had moved into her own apartment two years ago. Cindy had really helped Shelley from being lonely. Shelley was glad she and Cindy were friends. She reached over to give Cindy a sudden hug.

"I'm just crazy about you, you know?" Shelley clowned.

"Hey," Cindy protested, straightening a ruffle on her blouse, "don't wrinkle the cloth." They looked at each other and began to giggle.

Shelley's parents came across the parking lot and got into the car, smiling at the girls. "You two sound happy," Mr. Carter observed.

"When is it you leave for Europe?" Cindy asked. "It's right away, isn't it? My folks had a fit when I told them about it. Dad groaned and Mom turned absolutely green with envy."

"We leave Monday night," Shelley's father said over his shoulder. He started the car and drove it out of the church lot, turning toward home.

"We're not packed yet," Shelley's mother told Cindy. "I love Paris. I'm glad we're going again. There's so much I didn't have time to see when we went before." She turned to Shelley's father. "John, don't let me forget to pick up my shoes at the repair shop tomorrow. They're my best walking shoes. I'm having new heels put on them."

Shelley's father pulled into the driveway of their two-story brick home and stopped in front of the garage.

"Don't forget this is a business trip," he

said, getting out of the car. "I'll be in meetings all day, every day, for the full two weeks."

"I know. I plan to shop while you're in all those meetings," Shelley's mother said happily. She followed her husband to the house. "Don't worry, John. I won't be bored."

"Mom won't be bored, but I will," Shelley grumbled to Cindy. "I don't know why Dad's boss waited until school started to send him to Europe. If he'd gone last summer, I could have gone with them."

"I know how you feel," Cindy said sympathetically.

Shelley and Cindy started up the flagstone path to the kitchen door. Shelley's black and white cat sat on a low stone wall by the door, washing himself in the sunshine. Shelley picked him up.

"I wish my folks would let you stay at our house while they're gone," Cindy complained. "We'd have a blast."

"Mom says that's too much trouble for your parents," Shelley replied, planting a kiss on top of the cat's head.

Cindy shuddered, "How can you do that?" she asked. "Think of the germs."

"Oh, Bootsie doesn't have any germs," Shelley said. "He never has had."

"Good grief," Cindy groaned as she sat

down on the wall.

"I guess Mrs. White will stay with me again," Shelley said. "Mom and Dad have already talked to her about it. She's no fun. She's glued to the television all the time." Shelley sighed, thinking how long two weeks would seem with Mrs. White.

"Well, it could be worse," Cindy suggested. "Isn't Mrs. White the one who makes cookies every day?" She rolled her eyes and clutched her stomach as if she were starving. "I'll come over a lot, okay? I'm really into chocolate chips."

"There's more to life than food," Shelley said, refusing to laugh at Cindy. "Think how deadly dull it's going to be here." She put Bootsie back on the wall.

"Come on, Shelley, it's just for two weeks," Cindy argued. "Anyway, you'll be in school most of the time. And cheerleading practice takes a lot of time."

"That's true," Shelley said, feeling a little more cheerful. "Maybe we could work on our master plan to get Ted Hayes to notice that I'm alive. At least, we can talk on the phone more often with Mom not here to yell at me about it."

"Your mom doesn't yell," Cindy said.

"Oh, you know what I mean," Shelley told her.

Cindy nodded and smiled. Shelley and Cindy has already spent countless hours on their master plan. But their attempts to interest Ted in Shelley hadn't worked. Ted only lived across the street from Shelley. But Shelley hadn't made much of an impression on him. He seemed more interested in the new girl in school, Ashley Anderson.

"If only we had more classes together," Shelley said, frowning as she thought about it. "I really don't see Ted that much at school."

"Well, he just lives across the street. That helps," Cindy said. "And you have math class with him. One class has to be better than nothing."

"But Ashley has three classes with him," Shelley reminded Cindy.

"Shelley, you know Ashley isn't interested in Ted. She practically ignores him," Cindy said.

"Yes, and it just makes Ted that much more interested in her," Shelley said gloomily.

Cindy started to answer, but just then a small red car whipped into the driveway. "Who's that?" Cindy asked.

Shelley recognized her sister's new car. "It's Jackie," Shelley explained, waving. "That's her new car."

"When did she get a new car?" Cindy asked.

"She bought it a few weeks ago," Shelley

answered. "Dad gave her the down payment for her birthday."

Shelley ran down the path to meet her sister. Jackie swung out of the car just as Shelley got there. "I haven't seen you in weeks," Shelley said, hugging Jackie. "Where have you been?"

Jackie laughed, tossing her hair back. "Hey, I work, remember? And I'm taking night classes this term," she said. "I'm pretty busy."

"Classes?" Shelley cried. "Oh, Jackie, why didn't you tell us? Mom and Dad will be so pleased. You know how upset they were when you dropped out of college to go to work." She hugged Jackie again, excited.

Jackie shrugged. "I had to go to work if I wanted my own apartment," she said. "I can still finish college. I'll just do it my way. I had to go to work," she repeated. "I needed the money."

Jackie started toward the house. Shelley had to run to keep up with her. "Am I in time for dinner?" Jackie tossed back. "Oh, hi, Cindy," she added as she went past Cindy into the house.

"Hi," Cindy called to Jackie. "What's her big hurry?" she asked Shelley. "I can't remember ever seeing Jackie move that fast."

"She has good news for Mom and Dad,"

Shelley said. "She can't wait to tell them."

"Oh," Cindy replied. "Uh, shouldn't we go in and help your mother set the table or something?"

"Dinner's ready, girls," Shelley's mother called.

"I guess we're too late to set the table," Shelley said. "Come on, Cindy."

"We could offer to do the dishes," Cindy told her. "I mean, if Jackie's here, we won't be painting our nails or anything."

"What's the matter?" Shelley asked, staring at Cindy. "You're acting really weird, you know?"

"Well," Cindy said, "you and Jackie have always been so close."

"Do you feel left out?" Shelley asked, surprised. "Don't be dumb. You're my best friend. You know that. Let's go eat, okay? I'm starving."

Cindy grinned. "Me, too," she agreed.

Shelley and Cindy went inside and joined the others at the dining room table. Shelley shook out her napkin after she sat down and turned to her father. "Did Jackie tell you her news?" she asked.

"What news? Could you pass the salt, Shelley?"

Shelley handed the saltshaker over. "Come

on, Jackie, tell them," she coaxed.

"Well, it's just that I'm taking some classes," Jackie said, looking uncomfortable. "It's no big deal. I just thought I'd work toward my degree."

"Wonderful!" her father exclaimed.

"That's great, Jackie," her mother joined in. "But..."

"But what?" Jackie asked angrily. "What's wrong with taking some classes? Should I have asked permission first?"

Shelley couldn't believe Jackie had said that to her mother. Shelley looked at Cindy, but Cindy was staring at her plate.

"Jackie..." Jackie's father began.

"Hey, I'm sorry, okay?" Jackie interrupted. "I'm just tired. I'm not getting much sleep."

"That's what I started to ask you about, honey," her mother said. "I simply wonder if you might be trying to do too much. You haven't had your new job very long. Can you handle both?"

"I just need to go to bed earlier," Jackie muttered.

Her parents looked at each other. "That sounds like a good idea," her father said. "Say, I just thought of something. Would you like to stay here while we're gone? It would be a change for you, and Shelley would enjoy it."

Jackie looked surprised. "Where are you going?" she asked.

"I have a business trip coming up. We leave tomorrow. I haven't been able to reach you to tell you about it. We'll be in Paris again—for two weeks this time," her father said.

"That would work, John," Jackie's mother put in. "Jackie could pick Shelley up after cheerleading practice. Mrs. White will understand if we cancel. What do you think, Jackie?"

Jackie reached for the rolls. "Well, okay," she said. "Just remember, I don't make cookies."

"Great!" Shelley jumped up and gave Jackie a hug. "Oh, Mom, what a good idea," Shelley said, laughing. "It will be just like old times, won't it, Jackie?"

"Just like old times," Jackie agreed, buttering a roll.

"Then it's settled," her mother said, looking pleased. "I feel good about leaving with you here, Jackie," she added.

"Me, too," Shelley said quickly. She didn't mind being left behind if she could have Jackie staying with her.

"I have chocolate cake for dessert," Shelley's mother announced. "Is anyone interested?"

Cindy's face lit up. "Really? I feel a chocolate attack coming on," she said.

Everybody laughed.

Shelley had noticed that Cindy hadn't looked pleased when Jackie said she'd stay with Shelley. It doesn't matter if Cindy's a little jealous of my sister, Shelley thought happily. Cindy will get over it. And I'll have two whole weeks with Jackie. It's going to be wonderful. Shelley could hardly wait.

Two

MONDAY finally arrived. Shelley had been excited all day. She skipped cheerleading practice so she could be home when her mom and dad left for the airport. When she got off the school bus that afternoon, she expected to see Jackie's car in the driveway. But it wasn't there yet.

Shelley bounced into the house. Her parents' bags were all packed and sitting by the kitchen door. Her mother was watching the driveway through the window.

"Well, where's Jackie?" Shelley asked, disappointed. "She's supposed to be here by now, isn't she?"

"I don't know where she is," her mother answered. "Your dad's gone over to her apartment. We only have an hour until we have to leave for the airport."

"Why didn't Dad just call her?" Shelley asked.

"She didn't answer the phone, honey," her mother said. "I can't imagine what's happened." She bit her lip.

"Oh, don't worry, Mom," Shelley said quickly. "She'll get here."

"We can't get on that plane until we know that," her mother said. "I'm worried, Shelley. Jackie's always been so dependable. I'm afraid something may have happened to her. I can't understand why she isn't here."

"I hear the car in the driveway," Shelley said. She ran to the kitchen door and looked out. "It's Dad, but Jackie's not with him."

Shelley's father walked into the kitchen. He looked upset.

"John, did you find Jackie? Is she all right?" Shelley's mother asked.

Shelley's father poured a cup of coffee and leaned back against the counter. "She'll be here in ten minutes or so. I told her how inconsiderate her behavior was."

"Where was she? Where did you find her?" Shelley's mother asked.

Shelley's dad shrugged. "She was in her apartment. She said she fell asleep on the couch. I had to make a lot of noise to get her to answer the door. I'm lucky one of her neighbors didn't call the police, I guess."

"Didn't she hear the telephone?" Shelley asked.

"It was unplugged," her father said.

Shelley's mother still looked concerned. "John, you don't suppose she's sick, do you? Maybe you'd better go without me this time."

"How could she just fall asleep when she knew she was supposed to be here?" Shelley asked, confused.

"That's exactly what I wanted to know," her father said. "I don't think Jackie's sick. She told us she's been short on sleep lately. I think it's because of that gang of new friends she's seeing. They must stay up all night. No, we're going to Paris, Karen," he said to his wife. "Both of us are going. Jackie's okay."

"Well, if you're sure. . ." Shelley's mother began.

"Jackie's here," Shelley said. "I hear her car."

"See, there she is." Shelley's dad put down his coffee cup and gave Shelley a hug. "Be good, honey," he said. "And try to convince your sister she needs her rest, will you?" He dropped a kiss on the top of her head.

"I will, Dad," Shelley promised. "You and Mom have a good time, okay?"

Jackie came through the kitchen door. "Well, is it good-bye time?" she asked breezily. "Do I get a hug, too, or is anybody speaking to me?"

"Come here, Jackie," her father said, and gave her a big hug and a kiss.

"Oh, Jackie," her mother said as she hugged and kissed both girls, "you know we love you. You, too, Shelley."

"I'm really sorry I'm late, Mom," Jackie said, giving her mother a little push toward the door. "Don't miss your flight. Never fear, Jackie's here."

Her dad picked up the flight bags. "Come on, honey, we have to hurry," he said. "Good-bye, girls."

"Take care of each other," Shelley's mother called as the kitchen door closed behind them.

Jackie began rummaging in the refrigerator. "What do we have to eat in here?" she muttered, pulling food out. She stacked containers on the counter and opened the cabinets. "Oh, good, chocolate chip cookies," she said. She pulled out the cookies and a package of potato chips, too.

"Boy, for someone who was just sound asleep, you sure are wide awake now," Shelley said. "Say, where are your things? Did you bring a bag or something?"

Jackie snapped her fingers. "It's in my car," she said. She tore open a sack of potato chips and stuffed chips into her mouth. "I'm starving," she mumbled around the chips. "Would you get my bag for me?"

"Sure," Shelley said, and went out to the car.

By the time Shelley got back, her sister had set supper out on the table. Besides the cookies and potato chips, there were tortilla chips, salsa, onion dip, and a half dozen chocolate cupcakes with cream filling. Jackie was opening a liter of orange soda to go with the meal.

"That looks great," Shelley said. She laughed. "Mom would never let us eat junk food for supper if she were here."

"I know." Jackie grinned. "I'd rather have leftover pizza, but there isn't any." She giggled. "Listen, Shelley, when you're on your own, you'll do what you please, too. I eat hamburgers for breakfast and ice cream for supper if I want to. It's neat."

Shelley started to leave the kitchen. "I have to wash the jeans I have on for school tomorrow," she said. "I'm going to change into my pajamas before I eat. Do you want me to hang up your clothes in your old room?"

"I'll take care of that," Jackie said quickly.

She snatched the travel bag from Shelley's hand. "And I'll keep my room cleaned up. So you don't need to be in there at all, okay?"

"I've never bothered your things," Shelley said, hurt by what Jackie seemed to mean.

"I didn't say you had," Jackie told her calmly. "Look, I'll take care of my room, and you take care of yours. Then we'll share the rest of the housework. See? We can take turns doing the dishes, too," she went on, reaching for a plate. "If we keep things cleaned up, we won't be in a big rush to do it just before Mom and Dad get home."

Shelley stared at her sister. Maybe Jackie didn't mean it like it sounded, she thought. Maybe she just wants to take care of her own things. Shelley shrugged, and ran upstairs to her room. She changed into her pajamas. Then she went to the laundry room. She put her jeans in the washer and started the wash cycle.

Jackie had already eaten when Shelley got back to the kitchen. But she sat and talked while Shelley ate. Shelley laughed herself almost sick at the funny stories Jackie told her about her new job.

It was almost dusk when Shelley remembered to feed Bootsie. She fixed his bowl and stepped outside with it, thinking how neat it had been to have junk food for supper. She sat down on the wall to watch Bootsie eat.

Shelley looked across the yard at the blaze of fall flowers growing against the white wall of the garage. She remembered when she and Jackie had planted them.

Jackie came down the walk and sat on the wall beside Shelley. "We had a lot of fun the day we planted those flowers, didn't we?" Jackie asked. "Remember, we went to that awful movie after we got done? It was called 'Revenge of the Moon Monsters' or something like that."

Shelley began to grin. "I used up all my allowance to buy three big sacks of popcorn. Did I ever get sick!"

"And I took care of you until Mom and Dad got home from that school meeting," Jackie added. She flung her arm around Shelley's shoulder.

The cat jumped from the wall, stretched, and trotted off. Shelley stood up, looking at the sky. "It's a great evening, isn't it, Jackie?" she asked, taking a deep breath of cool air. "Listen, do you think what we ate for supper will make my face break out by morning?"

"Hi, there," a male voice called.

"Oh, hi, Ted," Jackie called back, waving. Ted Hayes was standing on the curb in front of his house. He had just put two trash bags out for pickup the next day. He was looking right at Shelley and Jackie.

Shelley darted into the house, red-faced. I can't stand it, she thought. Ted saw me in my pajamas. Shelley could hear Jackie outside joking with Ted. Of course, Jackie's too old for Ted, Shelley thought. But I'm not. And now he'll probably think I'm some dumb little kid, running around outside in pajamas.

Jackie came back into the kitchen, shutting the door behind her. "Ted's really grown up since I left home," Jackie said. "He's turned into a good-looking guy, you know?"

"I guess so," Shelley said, embarrassed. To change the subject, she added, "Ted's sister moved home again. I guess she got tired of apartment living. I think she and her boyfriend broke up, too, didn't they?"

"I wouldn't know," Jackie answered, not looking at Shelley. "I hardly ever see Ginny any more."

The telephone rang in the hall. "I'll get it," Shelley said, rushing into the hall. "Hello," she said into the phone.

"I'm blow-drying my hair," Cindy said breathlessly. "I can't talk."

Shelley giggled. "Then why did you call?" she asked.

"I want to know if I can borrow your blue

top," Cindy said. "Are you and your sister having a good time?"

"Oh, sure. We had the neatest supper! We had chips, and dip, and. . ."

"Will you bring the top with you to school tomorrow?" Cindy interrupted.

"Yes. Cindy, I'm really going to have a great time with Jackie here," Shelley rushed on. "This is so neat! Now that she's been out on her own, she's so. . ."

"I have to go," Cindy broke in again. "Mom says she'll bring you home after cheerleading practice tomorrow. She wasn't sure if Jackie would get home from work in time. Okay? Good-bye."

"Wait," Shelley cried.

"I have to go, Shelley," Cindy repeated.

"I have to tell you this awful thing that just happened with Ted," Shelley said, dropping her voice.

"I really do have to go. We can talk about it tomorrow. Don't forget the blue top," Cindy said, and hung up.

Shelley could hear Jackie singing in the kitchen over the clink of silverware and dishes. Jackie always used to sing around the house, Shelley remembered. The sound made Shelley happy.

Shelley ran to the laundry room to put her

jeans in the dryer. When she went back into the kitchen, she found it spotless. And she found Jackie putting on her jacket.

"Where are you going?" Shelley asked, surprised.

"I had a phone call," Jackie said. "I need to leave for a little while, okay?" She pulled her car keys out of her pocket.

"I thought we'd just sort of talk tonight," Shelley said, trying not to show how disappointed she felt.

"Hey," Jackie said, giving Shelley a hug. "I'll be here for two weeks, you know? We'll have lots of time to talk. I'll be back before you know it."

* * * * *

Jackie was gone for the rest of the evening. Shelley finally gave up waiting for her and went to bed.

When Shelley woke the next morning, she could hear Jackie downstairs in the kitchen fixing breakfast. Shelley got up, turned on the shower in the bathroom, and stepped in. Jackie just has to get used to being home again, she thought to herself. She won't be going out all the time.

By the time the bus picked Shelley up for

school, she'd forgotten all about Jackie's being gone the night before. She had more important things on her mind. Will Ted say anything in front of everybody on the bus about my pajamas? Shelley wondered. If he does, I'll just die, she thought. She made sure she sat as far away from him on the bus as she could get, just in case. But Ted didn't even look at her.

Three

L ATE Tuesday afternoon, Shelley climbed out of the Brooks' car in front of her house.

"Would you like me to bring you home after cheerleading practice tomorrow, too?" Cindy's mother asked, leaning out of the car window to peer up at Shelley.

"No, thanks, Mrs. Brooks," Shelley told her. "Jackie's going to pick me up until Mom and Dad get back."

"Jackie Jill went up the hill," Cindy's little brother Jimmy chanted from the front seat.

Shelley ignored Jimmy's remark. Sometimes, she and Cindy had agreed, that was all you could do. "Thanks a lot for the lift today, though," Shelley remembered to tell Mrs. Brooks.

"See you tomorrow," Cindy said.

"Jackie Jill, Jackie Jill," Jimmy shouted.

"James!" Mrs. Brooks pushed her glasses back up on her nose and glared at the little boy. Shelley giggled as they drove away. Jimmy was a pest, but he was cute. And Cindy's mother was funny when she was mad at him.

Shelley ran up the steps to the front door. Jackie's car was parked out front, so Shelley knew Jackie was home.

Shelley went inside the house. "Jackie? I'm here," she called. Jackie didn't answer.

Shelley took her gym bag to the laundry room and dumped its contents into the washer. She added detergent and punched the buttons to start the cycle.

Shelley went back through the kitchen and the dining room, but Jackie wasn't there. The house was quiet. "Jackie?" Shelley called again. She started up the stairs. Jackie has to be in her bedroom, Shelley thought.

Jackie's bedroom door was closed. Shelley saw that her sister had taken the hall phone into her bedroom. The cord was stretched under the door.

Shelley knocked on Jackie's door. "I'm home," she said, raising her voice. "Are you on the phone?"

"Go away," Jackie mumbled.

"What's the matter?" Shelley called,

puzzled. She turned the doorknob. Then she stared at the knob. The door was locked.

Shelley took a step back. She felt as if someone had hit her. Why did she do that? she wondered. Nobody would bother Jackie here. Nobody would even be here but me.

"Tired...Supper's on the stove...Need to sleep, okay?" Jackie said through the door.

"Don't you have a class tonight?" Shelley asked.

"Forgot...Doesn't matter," came the reply. "I'll be down later."

"Jackie?" Shelley called again.

There was no answer. Shelley went back down the stairs to the kitchen. A pot of thick soup sat on the stove. Shelley turned on the burner to warm it up. Then she found some cheese in the refrigerator and made a sandwich. She dished the soup, poured a glass of milk, and carried it all to the the table. She took a spoonful of soup, but she found she could hardly swallow it. Her throat was too tight.

Shelley looked through the double window at the sky. It was starting to get dark. "I might as well study," she said out loud. Shelley set out cat food for Bootsie and put her uneaten supper in the sink. Then she found her history book and curled up in her dad's big leather recliner chair in the living room.

It was almost time to go to bed when Shelley heard Jackie moving around in the kitchen. Shelley climbed out of the chair and went to talk to her sister. She found Jackie in her robe, staring at the soup pot on the stove.

"I forgot to put the soup in the refrigerator," Shelley apologized. "It's not spoiled, is it?"

Jackie shrugged and turned on the burner under the pot. Then she looked at Shelley's bowl in the sink. "You weren't hungry?" she asked. "Wasn't the soup okay?"

Shelley hesitated. "I couldn't eat," she said honestly. "You locked your door, and I didn't know what to think about it."

Jackie looked at Shelley with tears in her eyes.

"What's wrong, Jackie?" Shelley asked, alarmed. "Are you sick?"

Jackie slumped into a chair at the table. "I made the soup for you," she muttered. "I made it myself. You used to like my soup." She began to cry. "I'm so tired," she said.

"What's the matter? What is it?" Shelley begged.

"Don't worry," Jackie told Shelley. "I'm going back to bed. I'm just tired. I'll be fine in the morning. You'll see." Jackie fished a tissue from her pocket and blew her nose.

"See?" she said with a little smile. "I'm okay." She got up from the table and started for the hall.

Jackie stopped in the doorway. "Oh. I forgot. Mom and Dad called before you got home," Jackie said, as if it weren't especially important.

"Wait," Shelley cried. "What did they say?"

Jackie turned and looked at Shelley. "Well, they said they got there."

"Was that all?" Shelley asked.

"Let me think," Jackie said. "They like the hotel in Paris, I remember that. They want to know if we're taking care of each other. That's all."

"Oh," Shelley said, wishing she had been home for the call.

Jackie left the kitchen. Shelley heard her going upstairs.

Something smelled burned. Shelley ran across the room to the stove. Jackie hadn't turned off the burner, and the pot was scorched. Making a face, Shelley pushed the pan into the sink and filled it with water.

"Come on, Bootsie," Shelley said, snatching up the cat from the floor. "You're going to sleep with me tonight."

* * * * *

Shelley woke the next morning to find Bootsie standing on her pillow, purring. She could hear Jackie singing loudly in the shower. The sunlight falling through the windows was bright. It looked to Shelley like it would be another beautiful fall day.

Shelley dropped the cat to the floor and jumped out of bed. Since Jackie's singing, that must mean she's okay, Shelley thought. She felt relieved. She dashed down the stairs to the kitchen.

Shelley fixed Bootsie's dish and put it and the cat outside. Then she pulled frozen waffles from the freezer and got out the syrup. By the time Jackie came downstairs, breakfast for two was all done.

"Oh, great," Jackie said as she saw the food on the table. "This is one of my favorite breakfasts. Thanks, sis," she added, pulling out a chair.

Shelley sat down across the table from Jackie. She looked at her sister. There were faint shadows under Jackie's eyes, but she looked rested and cheerful. "Do you feel okay today?" Shelley said.

"Yes. I'm fine," Jackie said, pouring syrup over her waffles. "I sure slept well. I was beat last night."

"You must have been to forget to go to

class," Shelley said.

Jackie stopped eating and looked at Shelley. "Don't worry about it," she told her. "This is college. It's not like high school, you know. I can cut a class now and then."

"But you didn't cut it," Shelley said, confused. "You said you forgot to go. That's not the same thing."

Jackie shrugged. "It's no big deal. I needed the rest. I have a big day today at work. They're starting evaluations, and I need to be sharp." She looked at her watch.

"You'll pick me up after practice, won't you? You won't have to work late or anything?" Shelley asked.

"Oh, sure," Jackie said, throwing down her napkin. "I have to run. I'll see you this afternoon, okay? I'll be waiting outside the school, right in front."

* * * * *

When Shelley walked outside the school after cheerleading practice that afternoon, the red car wasn't there.

"Jackie will be here in a minute," Shelley told Cindy. "You go on home, okay?"

"Are you sure you don't want Mom to take you home?" Cindy asked. "It's going to rain."

"No. Jackie said she'd pick me up," Shelley said. "She'll be here. I don't want to miss her."

Shelley sat on the steps and watched the cars drive away one by one. After a while, she went into the school building. She called home, but there was no answer at the other end of the line. Shelley waited a few minutes and called again. There was still no answer.

Shelley wasn't sure what to do. She walked back outside and sat down on the steps again.

"I'm getting ready to lock up here," the janitor called from the door. "Do you want to make another phone call?"

"No, thanks," Shelley said politely. "That's okay." She stood up and slung her gym bag over her shoulder. I'll catch the city bus, she thought. Maybe Jackie will come along before the bus does.

Shelley walked down to the corner and watched for Jackie's car while she waited for the bus. It began to rain. By the time the bus arrived, Shelley was soaked. It was still raining when the bus pulled up to the stop two blocks from Shelley's house.

Shelley's teeth were chattering when she let herself in the front door. Jackie came into the living room from the hall and stopped, staring at Shelley. "I was just leaving to pick you up," she said quickly. "Why didn't you wait for me?"

"Thanks a lot," Shelley said. "Practice was over more than an hour ago. Where were you?"

"Oh, it can't be that late," Jackie scoffed. "I haven't been home from work that long."

Shelley pulled off her wet canvas shoes. "You just don't want to admit you forgot to pick me up," she said angrily.

"Okay, so I forgot," Jackie shouted. "Do you have to make a federal case out of it?"

Shelley looked at her sister. Then she ran up the stairs to her room. She changed her clothes. "I'd be better off if Mrs. White were here," she muttered, then felt guilty for thinking that. Maybe Jackie and I just aren't used to living together any more, Shelley thought. After all, she's been gone from home for two years.

Shelley had just started back downstairs to tell Jackie she was sorry she was so crabby, when the phone rang. Shelley ran back up a couple of steps to catch the phone in the upper hall. It was Cindy.

"Well, I guess Jackie picked you up," Cindy said. "I was just checking. I called earlier and didn't find anybody there."

"Hey, I'm home," Shelley said, feeling guilty all over again. But it's not a lie, she thought. "What do you need?" Shelley went on.

"Mom made at least a million cookies," Cindy said. "She thought she'd run a box over to your house. I guess she thinks you and Jackie are starving or something." Cindy giggled.

Shelley thought fast. The last thing she needed was for Cindy and her mom to show up when Shelley and Jackie had just had a fight. "Well. . . Can you bring them to school instead?" Shelley asked Cindy. "I can keep them in my locker until school's over. We're pretty busy," she added, crossing her fingers.

"Okay," Cindy said, sounding disappointed. "It's raining pretty hard, anyway. And it is kind of late, I guess."

"Tell your mom thanks a lot," Shelley said. "I'm sorry I wasn't home earlier." And that's the truth, Shelley thought. As she hung up the phone, she heard a door bang shut downstairs. She ran to her bedroom and looked out the window. Jackie's car was backing out of the driveway below.

"But she didn't even tell me she was leaving," Shelley said out loud, hurt. "I guess I should have told her I was sorry."

Four

BY the time Shelley got to gym class Friday afternoon, she was ready for school to be over. Gym class always seemed much worse on Friday than any other day. But today Shelley didn't care. She worked through the floor exercises without even thinking of them. She was too busy thinking about how things were at home.

Jackie had started to get phone calls late at night. Shelley had climbed out of bed the first few times to answer the phone. But when she found the calls were always for Jackie, she had stopped getting up. At least Jackie had picked Shelley up on time Thursday afternoon. But she'd just dropped Shelley off at home and left again.

Shelley was glad it was Friday. She had made up with Jackie after their fight, but it hadn't helped much. She and Jackie were being far too polite to each other and the strain was beginning to get to Shelley. She wasn't sure how well she'd done on her history test that morning, and it upset her.

I might as well be staying by myself, Shelley thought. Jackie's hardly ever home—and when she is, she's on the phone. She's just so busy. Maybe she'll have time for me this weekend. Maybe I'll talk to her about Ted.

"One, two. . . one, two. . . one, two and stop. All right, girls, take a break," Mrs. Jordan shouted. Groans sounded through the gym as a sea of 40 white T-shirts and blue shorts dropped to the floor. "Keep the noise down," the teacher called.

Shelley pulled her hair up off her hot neck. "The woman's a monster," she whispered. "Doesn't she ever get tired?"

"Nope," Cindy panted. "She doesn't even sweat."

"Neither does Ashley," Shelley added, turning to look at Ashley Anderson. "That's unreal. There's not a blonde hair out of place."

"I know. Don't you hate it?" Cindy whispered. "I'll bet she bleaches it, though."

Shelley nudged Cindy to keep still just as Mrs. Jordan started talking again. "I know you're all bored with exercises," the teacher said. A grumble of agreement rose about her.

She blew her whistle sharply, and the noise died down. "So for the next six weeks, we'll be doing aerobic dance." She grinned. "Don't worry, you'll like it."

"I can't believe she said that," Cindy said blankly. "That's hard work."

"Shhh," Shelley whispered as Mrs. Jordan looked toward Cindy.

"We'll be working on improving your exercise pulse rate," Mrs. Jordan went on. "I'll have charts for you to keep starting next Monday. Right now, I'm going to show you the basic routine so you'll know what to expect."

Mrs. Jordan walked quickly over to the bleachers. She flipped on the tape player Shelley had noticed earlier. The beat of music swelled into the gym as Mrs. Jordan began the routine. "Follow me, girls," she called. "Everybody up."

Shelley jumped to her feet with the rest of the class. She watched Mrs. Jordan to catch the rhythm, and then tried to follow the teacher's steps.

"I can't do this," Cindy gasped, bumping into Shelley. All the other girls were having trouble following the routine, too. . .all but Ashley. She was doing the steps perfectly. And she looked as if she enjoyed it.

"Look at Ashley," Shelley whispered to Cindy.

"I can't. I'll fall down," Cindy replied, but she threw a glance at Ashley. "I can't stand it," Cindy said. She missed a turn and nearly knocked Shelley over.

The music stopped. Mrs. Jordan blew her whistle. "Get rested over the weekend, girls," she called. "In six weeks you'll all do this as well as Ashley." She smiled at the chorus of denials that rose from the group. "Time for showers," the teacher shouted over the noise.

Shelley and Cindy ran across the floor toward the shower room with the other girls. "I think I'm dying," Cindy groaned. "Why is Mrs. Jordan doing this to us?"

"Oh, we'll learn how to do it," Shelley told Cindy. "I mean, all the cheerleading practice ought to help us. But I'll bet we won't learn to do it as well as Ashley does. . .not in just six weeks. Why does she have to be so perfect? I'm depressed."

"So what else is new?" Cindy asked, shrugging. "You've been depressed since Wednesday."

"I have not," Shelley denied.

"You have, too," Cindy said firmly. "You haven't even noticed I had my hair cut. And you haven't said a word about Ted for two whole days," she added, dropping her voice.

"When did you have your hair cut?" Shelley

asked, surprised at herself.

"See?" Cindy said. "I had it done Wednesday night, and this is Friday. You're slipping."

"Well, you didn't have that much cut off," Shelley said. "And besides, I've been studying for that history test."

"Who hasn't?" Cindy asked. "Is everything okay with you? I mean..."

"Sure," Shelley interrupted. "Everything's fine. Come on, we'll be late for math class." She ran ahead of Cindy through the doors to the shower room.

Some of the girls, already dressed, pushed out past Shelley on their way to their next classes. Shelley went straight to her locker and pulled out her towel without waiting for Cindy to catch up. She was glad the shower room was always so noisy. It made it hard to hear in there. And Shelley was afraid Cindy might start asking more questions.

Shelley turned on the water and then stepped into the shower. She cooled off quickly under the soothing water pouring over her shoulders. She wanted to tell Cindy that things weren't exactly right at home. But Cindy was already jealous of Jackie. Shelley was sure Cindy wouldn't understand.

There really isn't anything wrong anyway,

Shelley thought. It's just that Jackie's not like she used to be. That doesn't mean there's anything wrong. It has to be because she's been out on her own, Shelley reasoned, feeling better.

Shelley jumped out of the shower and dried off. She dressed quickly. The locker room was empty, and she didn't want to be late for math class. Ted was in that class with her. She'd be embarrassed to walk in late.

Cindy rushed into the room just as Shelley zipped up her jeans. "What took you so long?" she asked.

Shelley didn't answer. She picked up her books and headed for the hall with Cindy behind her.

"Ted's hanging around the door to the math room," Cindy said, looking excited. She skipped to keep up with Shelley's longer legs. "That's why I came back after you," she said. "This is your chance. Think of something brilliant to say when you go past him."

"Like what?" Shelley asked, feeling panic in the pit of her stomach.

"Oh, anything," Cindy insisted. "Ask him if he put out the trash this morning. I don't know. You think of something. You're the honor roll student, not me."

"He doesn't even know I'm alive," Shelley

said. "He didn't say anything about seeing me in my pajamas. I really thought he'd make a joke about it. I'm glad he didn't, though," she added.

"I'd have just died," Cindy agreed.

The girls rounded the corner. Ted was leaning against the wall by the classroom door. And Ashley, looking like she'd just stepped out of the pages of *Miss Teen*, was smiling up at him.

"Well," Cindy said blankly, "there goes our master plan. I thought she wasn't interested in Ted."

"I guess she changed her mind," Shelley said. "Come on." She marched toward the door, determined to look perfectly normal. "Hi, Ted," Shelley said clearly. "Oh, hi, Ashley." She threw back over her shoulder as she went by them through the door.

Shelley saw Cindy's admiring glance as they took their seats, but Shelley ignored it. She was angry. She was angry with Ted because he didn't pay any attention to her. And she was angry with Jackie, too, for not being like she used to be. It was all mixed up together, somehow. Shelley hated feeling like that.

Math class and the next class passed quickly, and so did cheerleading practice. Almost before Shelley realized it, she was on the school steps waiting for Jackie.

"Call me tomorrow," Cindy said as she got into her mother's car. "Maybe we can do something together, okay?"

Shelley saw Jackie's little red car coming up the street. "Maybe," she answered Cindy. Shelley was thankful that she wouldn't have to take the city bus home tonight. The thought made her angry all over again. When Jackie pulled up, Shelley threw her gym bag in the backseat. Then she got into the car, slamming the door.

"Hey, don't break it," Jackie teased. "It's not paid for yet. Did you have a bad day, sis?"

Shelley started to answer, but Jackie was still talking. "Why don't we grab a sandwich on campus for supper?" Jackie suggested. "Would you like to come to class with me tonight?"

Shelley looked at her sister. "I'd like that," she said slowly. "Are you sure you want me?"

"Sure," Jackie said, putting the car in gear. "We used to have a lot of fun together, remember? And when we finish the grocery shopping tomorrow, how about a movie? But you have to promise not to get sick on popcorn," she added, giggling.

"That sounds like fun," Shelley said without thinking.

"Good," Jackie said.

"I could use a triple cheeseburger and a shake," Shelley said. "They had beans in the cafeteria at noon. Yuck."

Jackie began to laugh, and before long, Shelley was laughing, too. Everything's just fine again, Shelley thought. Oh, I'm glad Jackie's home.

Five

THE college on the other side of town was small, but it was a good one. Shelley noticed the old brick buildings glowed pink in the late afternoon sunlight. As she had expected, the campus was beautifully leafed in fall's gaudy colors.

After Jackie's anthropology lecture, Shelley and Jackie walked through the campus. Drifts of yellow leaves lay to the sides of the pebbled path. They entered the Commons and stood in line for something to drink while they talked. When Jackie found a table for them, a couple of students drifted over. One of them began telling about his field trip last summer. He was hilarious. Shelley couldn't remember when she had laughed so hard.

* * * * *

Shelley slept like a log Friday night. After she got up Saturday morning, she mowed the yard while Jackie straightened up the house. Then the two of them set off for the supermarket to do the grocery shopping. Jackie was as cheerful as she'd been the night before. The sky was clear and blue, the sun was warm, and Shelley was happy. She giggled all the way to the store. Jackie threatened to make her walk if she didn't stop.

When the girls reached the supermarket, Shelley went after cat food and paper products. Jackie wheeled the cart toward the fruit and vegetable section. By the time Shelley found her, the cart was nearly full.

"Are you into vegetables or what?" Shelley asked, poking through the cart. "I had fried chicken in mind. Avocados? An eggplant? Mom never fixes eggplant."

Jackie grinned. "I'm not a beef-and-noodles cook, you know."

"I hadn't thought of you as a cook," Shelley said frankly. "You never made anything much but brownies when you lived at home. What's that?" she asked as Jackie dropped another plastic bag into the cart.

"That's for you. It's kiwi fruit," Jackie explained. "I'm broadening your horizons."

"I like the horizons I have. . .Oh, hi,

Mrs. White," Shelley interrupted herself to say. When she turned back, Jackie had piled pickles, olives, and chip dip into the cart. "I'm glad you're staying with me for these two weeks," Shelley said. "Not that Mrs. White isn't a nice person. Isn't this fun?"

"Pick up a couple of liters of soft drinks," Jackie told Shelley. "I think that's all we need now."

Shelley put the bottles on the bottom shelf of the shopping cart. "What's all this for?" she asked.

"I thought we'd stay up to watch the late movie on television tonight," Jackie said. "This is for munchies during the show."

"That sounds good," Shelley said, puzzled. "But we're going to catch a movie this afternoon. Isn't that a lot of movies for one day? I thought we'd have time to just talk."

"I've seen all the films playing in town," Jackie replied. "I checked the titles. Sorry."

"Oh," Shelley said. "Well, we can still talk."

Jackie plucked a big package of chips from the shelf as she pushed the cart toward a check-out line. "Isn't that Ted over there by the magazine rack?" she asked.

"Where?" Shelley gasped. "Oh, no. Ashley's talking to him."

"Oh, look. There's Ted's mother, too. Hello

Mrs. Hayes," Jackie called.

Shelley felt her face get hot. "Jackie, shhh," she whispered.

"What's the matter?" Jackie said returning Mrs. Hayes' wave. "Who's that girl with them?"

"Oh, she's just a new girl at school," Shelley mumbled. "You don't know her."

"Hi, Jackie. Hi, Shelley." Ginny Hayes, Ted's sister, waved and came toward them. "I haven't seen you for a long time, Jackie," she went on. "What's new with you?"

Jackie didn't answer. She started unloading the contents of the shopping cart onto the check-out counter.

Well, say something, Shelley thought to herself, staring at Jackie.

"I'm really in kind of a hurry," Jackie finally said, without looking at Ginny.

Shelley couldn't believe it. Ginny and Jackie used to be good friends. They must have had a fight or something, Shelley thought. "How's college?" Shelley asked quickly, trying to make conversation.

"Fine. It's going really well," Ginny said, turning to Shelley. "I suppose you know I just moved back home last week. I meant to come over and visit your folks, but Mom says they've gone to Europe. I'll catch them when they get home."

"Oh, they'd like that," Shelley said.

"Are you staying with Shelley right now?" Ginny asked Jackie.

"That's right," Jackie answered coldly.

Ginny flushed. "Well, I'll see you later, I guess. Take care, Shelley," she said. She turned to join her mother in the next check-out line.

Red-faced, Shelley slid past Jackie and headed for the doors. She had to get away. She got into Jackie's car and waited for her sister.

Jackie loaded the groceries into the trunk of the car and got in. "What's wrong with you and Ginny?" Shelley asked. "You were really rude to her. Have you had a fight?"

Jackie shrugged. "It has nothing to do with you," she said.

"We're neighbors," Shelley argued.

"We're just not close any more," Jackie said. "People change, you know."

"Ginny hasn't changed," Shelley said.

"I have a great idea," Jackie said. "There's a new store a couple of blocks away. Would you like to check it out with me? You could use a new top, couldn't you?"

"I don't have any money," Shelley said.

"You don't need any," Jackie told her. "I'm buying."

"Really?" Shelley was surprised and pleased. "Do you think you have enough for a burger and fries, too? she asked.

"Good grief," Jackie said, laughing. "Where do you put all that food?"

Shelley just smiled. She was excited about looking for a new top. "You'll help me pick my top out, won't you?" she asked. "What about the groceries?"

"They won't spoil. I didn't buy anything that will melt," Jackie said. "Let's find you a gorgeous top, okay?"

* * * * *

Shelley had so much fun shopping that she forgot about Ginny. She and Jackie sang in the car going home. And when they ran out of camp songs, they laughed at old jokes.

Shelley was so pleased with the pink top she'd found that she turned down the burger and fries she'd wanted. She had a salad instead, and felt very virtuous about it.

It was almost dark when the two girls reached home. They carried the groceries into the house and began putting them away in the kitchen.

"It's been a great day, hasn't it?" Shelley said, looking out the double window. Slanting sunlight gleamed on the dark green shrubbery across the back of the yard. Shelley admired the freshly mowed lawn. She sighed happily and finished folding the paper bags they'd emptied.

"You bet," Jackie agreed. She tossed the cash register receipt into the wastebasket. Then she retrieved it. "Mom might want this," she said.

The phone rang in the hall. "That's Cindy," Shelley guessed out loud, racing to answer it.

"Jackie there?" It was a man's voice—one Shelley didn't know.

"May I say who's calling?" Shelley asked politely.

"Tell her it's Skipper," the voice said, sounding impatient.

Shelley put down the phone and went to tell Jackie it was for her.

Jackie went to the phone. While she took her call, Shelley took Bootsie's supper outside for him. She stopped to stroke his sleek fur and laughed as he rolled around in the grass. When Shelley went back into the house, Jackie was pouring cola over ice in two glasses.

"Oh, thanks," Shelley said, picking up one of the glasses. "Jackie, what's this movie you want to watch tonight?" She took a big drink of the cola.

"Well. . .I've changed my mind," Jackie said, "I'm not going to watch it."

Shelley put down her glass, surprised. "But you bought all that food to eat during the movie," she reminded Jackie.

"Someone may drop by tonight," Jackie said, not looking at Shelley.

"Oh," Shelley said. She felt disappointed. "I suppose it's Skipper—the guy that called here, right? Is anybody else coming?"

"Just a few friends," Jackie said, "nobody you know." She hesitated. "I need to run up to my room for just a minute. If anybody else calls, get a name and tell them I'll call back. Okay?" Jackie darted from the room before Shelley could answer.

The phone rang again. Shelley picked it up. She heard a husky girl's voice in her ear. "Jackie? Is it on?"

"This is her sister," Shelley said. "She can't come to the phone right now."

"Just tell her I'll call Tom and Ricky. And have her call me back. Okay? I'm Jo Ellen." And she hung up.

Shelley stared at the phone. Who is Jo Ellen? she wondered. Why doesn't Jackie get calls from her old friends—friends that I know, too?

When Jackie came downstairs, Shelley was definitely not in a good mood. "Some girl with a weird voice called," Shelley told Jackie. "She said her name was Jo Ellen. You're supposed to call her back."

Jackie started for the phone. Shelley followed

53

her into the hall. "What am I supposed to do when all these strangers show up?" she demanded. "Should I just stand around and look dumb?"

"You could try to be polite," Jackie told her. "Or is that too much to ask?" She pushed her hair back from her face with a quick angry gesture. "Do you mind?" she asked. "This is a private call I'm about to make."

"Excuse me," Shelley cried. "I didn't know we had secrets from each other." She whirled and ran from the hall. She stared at her dad's chair in the living room. She wanted very badly to call Cindy. She wanted to talk to her—not about Jackie, just about anything.

The phone rang again, and Shelley ignored it. It'll be more of Jackie's strange friends, she thought. Then she heard Jackie's voice—louder than it should be. "Sure, great. No, we're both fine, Dad. Do you want to speak to her?"

Shelley rushed into the hall and grabbed the phone from Jackie.

"Are you. . .good time, honey?" Shelley's father asked through the crackle of a poor connection.

"I wish you and Mom were here," Shelley said. "I miss you."

"What? Business is going well. . .We may have a chance to come. . .Can't hear very well.

Take care...selves. Love you."

"I love you, too, Dad," Shelley said. She put the silent receiver down carefully as the doorbell rang.

"I'm not going to answer the doorbell, Jackie," Shelley said. "It won't be anybody I know."

Jackie's face twisted briefly. She started to say something and then stopped. Shelley watched her sister walk away. She almost called her back. Maybe I'm wrong about Jackie's friends, she thought. After all, I haven't met them yet.

Shelley could hear voices talking and laughing in the living room. Jackie's probably right, she thought. It won't hurt me to be polite. Anyway, it's just one evening out of two weeks.

With that thought in mind, Shelley went into the living room. Six pairs of eyes looked at her from faces she'd never seen before. "Is that the kid sister?" one of the faces said, looking bored.

Six

AT three the next morning, Shelley gave up. There was no way she could sleep— not with all the noise going on downstairs. She crawled out of bed and went to look out her window. Windows began to light up in the Gerbers' house across the driveway.

A burst of laughter and cheering sounded through Shelley's house. Shelley shrank back from the window. Jackie's friends—in the kitchen now, from the sound of it—were laughing because they'd seen the neighbors' lights coming on. What will the Gerbers' think? Shelley wondered uneasily.

Shelley had tried to be polite to Jackie's new friends. She fixed snack trays for them and poured soft drinks. She even tried to talk to them, but they didn't seem interested in anything Shelley had to say. They drifted away from her like the smoke from their cigarettes.

Shelley finally told Jackie she was going to bed.

"You don't like my party?" Jackie had asked, giggling and talking so fast that the words all blurred together. "Have a cola. Oh, you already have one. Well, have another." Jackie must have thought that was funny. She kept laughing. Disgusted, Shelley had gone upstairs to her room. She'd had to step over a couple people sitting on the landing talking to each other. Oddly enough, the couple hadn't seemed to notice that Shelley had to practically climb over them to get past.

Shelley looked out the window again. Now the lights were coming on in the Hayes house across the street. In the glow of the streetlight, Shelley could see Ted's father on his porch. He was wearing his bathrobe, and he looked furious. He stared at Shelley's house and then went back into his own.

Shelley's face felt hot. She felt so embarrassed that she couldn't move. It's bad enough that Jackie's party woke up the Gerbers, she thought. But now Ted's father is upset, too. And Ted—what will Ted think? "I can't stand it," Shelley said out loud. "Ted will probably never speak to me again."

Mr. Hayes had come back out of his house. Fully dressed now, he started across the street.

"Oh, no," Shelley gasped. She flung her robe on and ran down the stairs and into the kitchen. There were a lot more people than there had been before. And they were all talking loudly. Shelley pushed her way through, looking for Jackie.

Jackie sat at a table, staring into a glass full of ice cubes. Shelley grabbed her sister's shoulder.

"Mr. Hayes is coming over here," Shelley cried above the noise. "Do something, Jackie."

Jackie looked up at Shelley, smiling dreamily.

"Mr. Hayes is coming," a voice mocked. "Oh, dear."

Shelley whirled to see a grinning face. It was the same one that had called her the kid sister when the crowd had started gathering. Shelley suddenly hated the face. "Why don't you all go home?" she shouted. "Just get out, okay?"

"Temper, temper," someone drawled at Shelley's shoulder.

"Jackie, do something," Shelley begged.

The doorbell rang, but nobody seemed to hear it. "That's Mr. Hayes. He's here," Shelley said. Jackie looked at Shelley as if she couldn't understand what Shelley was saying. The doorbell rang again and again.

"All right, I'll answer it," Shelley said loudly,

not knowing what else to do. "But you'd better tell all these people to leave before somebody calls the police."

"Police?" a voice said, startled.

"Is that the police?" another hissed. "Hey, I'm gone, you hear?"

"Let's split, Dodie," a tall girl cried.

Shelley ignored them all and ran out of the room. The kitchen door began banging behind her, and she could hear cars starting up in the driveway. It sounded as if the party had begun to break up. Shelley was too worried about facing Mr. Hayes to feel relieved. Shaking, she pulled the front door open.

"What in the world is going on in here?" Mr. Hayes rumbled, scowling. "Do you know what time it is?"

"Yes, sir," Shelley said, swallowing hard. "I'm sorry, Mr. Hayes. Everyone's leaving now."

"I thought your sister was more responsible than this. What do you think your parents would say?" Mr. Hayes persisted.

"I'm sorry," Shelley repeated hopelessly. I know exactly what they would say, she thought. And I have a feeling Mr. Hayes intends to tell them all about this as soon as they get home.

Tires squealed as another car left the

driveway for the street.

"I think you and Jackie had better go to bed, and let the rest of us get some sleep," Mr. Hayes warned.

"Yes, sir. I'm sorry, Mr. Hayes," Shelley called after him as he left the porch. She closed the door and locked it. Then she picked her way across the quiet room. There were glasses and plates on the floor. A forgotten guitar lay in her father's chair. Shelley pushed it out of the chair angrily. The guitar twanged as it hit the carpet, and a girl lying on the couch lifted her head to look at it.

"It's time to go home. The party's over," Shelley said. She walked past the couch and straight up the stairs to her room. I don't want to talk to Jackie, she thought. I just want to go to sleep and forget all this.

* * * * *

Somewhere a phone was ringing. Shelley opened her eyes to see that the sun was high in the sky. When she rolled over to look at her clock, it said twelve-thirty. She pushed herself up and out of bed, and padded barefoot into the hall.

The phone wasn't on its stand. Shelley tracked the cord into Jackie's room and picked up the receiver. "Hello?" she said.

"Boy, do you sound sleepy," Cindy answered. "I missed you at church. Did you sleep right through it?"

"Oh. . .Well, I guess so," Shelley said, remembering it was Sunday. She walked back into the hall and put the phone on the table. Cindy kept talking, but Shelley wasn't listening. Instead, she stared through Jackie's bedroom door at the bed. The door wasn't locked. And the bed didn't look as if it had been slept in.

"Shelley, didn't you hear me?" Cindy asked. "Say something."

"What do you want me to say?" Shelley answered. A feeling of dread began to turn her fingers cold. She remembered how funny Jackie had been acting last night. Where's Jackie now? she wondered.

"Well, say yes, of course," Cindy said crossly.

"Yes," Shelley said, trying to concentrate. "What did I just say yes to?"

Cindy snorted. "You're still asleep. I just told you Mom's going to take us to the movie at the mall this afternoon."

"What's playing?" Shelley asked, stalling.

"Disney reruns, of course," Cindy said with a sigh. "I told Mom I'd take Jimmy if you'd come, too. I told you all that once. Do you and Jackie have any plans, or can you go with me?"

"I don't know..." Shelley began.

"I don't want to hear it," Cindy broke in. "I can't sit through all those cute little bunnies and talking mice and things without you. We'll pick you up at two. And you be ready."

The receiver clicked in Shelley's ear. She put it down and ran to her room. She looked down at the driveway through her window. Jackie was bouncing out of her car carrying a white paper sack.

Shelley took a deep shaky breath. She rushed down the stairs and into the kitchen.

"Sleepyhead," Jackie crowed, waving the sack at Shelley. "Look, I have fresh doughnuts."

Shelley stared at her sister. Jackie looked perfectly okay now.

"I had to go to the bakery," Jackie said, laughing. "I can't let Jo Ellen starve. And you like doughnuts."

"Jo Ellen's coming over?" Shelley asked. "Haven't you had enough company lately? After last night..."

"No, she's not coming over, silly. She slept on the couch," Jackie said, pulling a tray from a drawer. She began placing doughnuts on it.

"Great party," Jo Ellen drawled. She stood in the doorway, eyeing the doughnuts. She yawned and stretched. It was obvious to Shelley that she'd slept in her clothes.

"What are you doing here?" Shelley asked.

Jo Ellen shrugged. "Rick took off without me. It's no big deal. Jackie's crashed at my place before." She sauntered to the table and sat down.

"When?" Shelley asked. "Why would Jackie stay at your place when she has her own apartment?"

Jo Ellen bit into a doughnut, watching Shelley. "Little Shelley's full of questions, isn't she?" she remarked.

"Oh, here. Drink your coffee and stop picking on Shelley," Jackie said. She laughed and handed Jo Ellen a cup of coffee. "Is Rick coming back for you?"

Jo Ellen nodded. "I called and told him to. He's bringing Terry along."

Oh, no, Shelley thought, dismayed. Is Sunday going to be as bad as Saturday night was?

Jo Ellen was still talking. "Nice house," she told Jackie, looking around. "Your couch is really comfortable."

Shelley couldn't keep still. "It *was* a nice house," she said loudly.

Jo Ellen raised her eyebrows. "Little Shelley has claws," she said.

Don't call me little Shelley, Shelley thought. "If there's another party here today, Jackie, Mr. Hayes will come back—or call the police," she said.

"Mr. Hayes?" Jackie looked surprised. "What does he have to do with anything?"

"You don't remember?" Shelley asked. "He was here at three this morning. I think he's going to tell Mom and Dad about last night."

"You're making that up," Jackie said. She scowled. "Anyway, it was just a little party. We weren't bothering anyone."

Jo Ellen put down her cup. "I don't think the kid's lying," she said. "I sort of remember some guy showing up at the door."

"I told you," Shelley said. "I told you last night that Mr. Hayes was on his way over here."

Jackie looked uncomfortable. "Okay," she said. "So Mr. Hayes came over. So what?"

"So you can't have another party here," Shelley insisted.

"Let's go to my place when Rick shows up," Jo Ellen suggested. She reached for another doughnut.

"But what would I do with Shelley?" Jackie asked. "This is Sunday. She's not in school."

"You're not asking what I want to do," Shelley said. "Don't I get a vote in my own home?"

"Shelley. . ." Jackie began, but Shelley interrupted her, feeling hurt.

"Don't worry about me," she said. "I already have plans for this afternoon. You're not my babysitter, you know."

Shelley stormed up the stairs to her room and slammed the door shut behind her. She managed to keep from crying until she was safely there. She heard Jackie and Jo Ellen come up the stairs and into Jackie's room. Then she heard the click of the lock on Jackie's door. The sound made Shelley even more miserable.

She might as well be locking me out of her life, Shelley thought. Don't I count anymore? She blew her nose, and wondered why Jackie had even agreed to stay with her while her parents were gone.

Shelley started to put on her new top. Then she looked at it and shoved it into a drawer. She didn't feel like wearing it. It reminded her of how much fun she'd had with Jackie the day before. Shelley dressed quickly and watched from her window for Cindy.

When Cindy's car pulled into the driveway, Shelley ran quickly down the stairs and out the door. She didn't want Cindy to come into the house after her. She didn't want her to meet Jo Ellen.

"Where's Jackie Jill?" Jimmy piped up as Shelley climbed into the backseat with Cindy.

"Would Jackie like to come along?" Cindy's mother asked. "I should have thought of that."

"Oh, no. That's all right," Shelley told her. "Jackie has something else to do."

"Quick, look," Cindy whispered. "There's Ted in his yard."

Shelley twisted around in the seat. Ted was clipping the shrubbery across the front of his house. He saw the girls looking at him and grinned, waving at them. Cindy returned the wave, but Shelley scooted down in the seat, suddenly shy. She was sure Mr. Hayes had told Ted about coming over to break up the party last night. What a mess, she thought.

"Are you okay?" Cindy whispered. "Why didn't you wave at Ted?"

"Oh, I don't know," Shelley said. She began talking about school. Soon Cindy was giggling, and Shelley breathed more easily. She didn't want Cindy to find out that she and Jackie weren't getting along. And she especially didn't want Cindy to know about last night. Shelley just wanted this week to be over. And she wanted her parents to come home.

Seven

S HELLEY plopped down on the bleachers, panting. It was Monday, and fifth period gym class was just ending.

"Good grief," puffed Cindy, red-faced. "I just don't think this is going to work. I can't keep up with those steps." She checked her pulse, and wrote it down in her chart. "Did anybody ever fail pulse rate?" she wondered aloud. "I'll bet I'll be the first to do it."

Breathlessly, Shelley nodded. She recorded her pulse rate and then stood up. "Come on," she said. "Let's get our walking lap done."

Cindy stopped swinging her arms. The two girls joined the rest of the class doing a slow lap around the gym. "Remember, breathe in, blow it out," Cindy said.

Shelley nodded again, only half listening. She was thinking about the day before. Cindy's mother had taken them all out for pizza after the movie. When Shelley had arrived back home, it was late. The house was dark. And when Shelley let herself in, she found Jackie sprawled on the floor in the living room, asleep. Frightened, Shelley shook Jackie awake. But Jackie didn't answer Shelley's questions. Instead, Jackie staggered up the stairs to her room.

Shelley had lain awake in bed, worrying about her sister. She heard Jackie crying, and went to her sister's door. It was locked, and Jackie didn't answer when Shelley knocked.

Shelley went back to her room. After what seemed like hours, she finally fell asleep. Even though Jackie had insisted she was just fine this morning, Shelley hadn't been able to think of anything else all day.

"Shelley!" Cindy said loudly.

Shelley looked around. Cindy was standing ten feet behind her, with her hands on her hips. "Are you planning to do another lap?" Cindy asked. "Your pulse rate must be down by now. Write it down, and let's go. Do you want to be late for math class?" She headed toward the shower room doors without waiting for a reply.

Shelley sighed. She noted her pulse rate and followed Cindy. She worried about Jackie again as she showered. Something's really wrong with Jackie, Shelley thought. But Jackie won't tell me what it is. She just keeps telling me everything's all right, when it's not.

Shelley dried off quickly and dressed. I'll talk to Jackie about it tonight, Shelley thought. I'll just tell her I'm her sister, and I have to know what's wrong. I don't know anything else to do.

Shelley looked around for Cindy, but she'd already dressed and gone to the next class. Shelley pushed through the doors and out into the hall, dodging a group of students.

"Whoa," a voice called. Ted caught Shelley's arm as she rushed by him. "Hey, why didn't you ask me over Saturday night?"

"What?" Shelley gasped.

"Dad said you had quite a bash going on," Ted joked. "It sounded like a party and a half. Was that your idea, or Jackie's?"

"I...I..." Shelley stammered. "I'm sorry."

"Sorry about the noise? Or sorry you didn't ask me to the party?" Ted asked. He was still holding Shelley's arm.

Shelley didn't know what to say. "I'll be late for math class," she managed to get out.

Ted grinned. "I'll walk you there," he said.

Shelley's face felt hot. She hadn't been sure she could even face Ted in math class after Saturday night. And this just made it worse. Is he interested in me, or is he just teasing? Shelley wondered. She wished he hadn't brought up the party. She hated even thinking about it. And she hoped Ted didn't think the party had been her idea.

Shelley saw Cindy's eyes widen as Shelley and Ted came into class together. Ashley glared at Shelley all through class. Shelley was too upset to be pleased that Ashley was mad.

The rest of the school day passed with agonizing slowness. Shelley told her cheerleading advisor that she didn't feel well so she could skip practice. Then she got on the school bus and took a seat next to a girl she hardly knew. She didn't want to leave an empty seat beside her. What if Ted took that seat. All I want to do right now is get home, Shelley thought. I have to talk to Jackie. I'll think about Ted later.

Jackie looked surprised to see Shelley walk through the kitchen door. "You should be at practice," she exclaimed. She turned from the stove where she was stirring a pot. "How did you get here?"

"I took the bus home," Shelley told her, putting her gym bag down.

"Oh. Why did you do that?" Jackie asked.

"How would I know you'd remember to pick me up after practice?" Shelley asked. "After that party Saturday night. . ."

"Come on," Jackie scoffed. "Don't be weird. It was just a little party. It was no big deal." She turned back to the stove. "I'm making chili," she went on. She tasted the chili.

"What happened to the avocados and the eggplant?" Shelley asked. "You told me you don't cook ordinary meals any more."

"We ate all that up Saturday night," Jackie said. She reached up into the cabinet. "This needs more chili powder," she went on.

"Ted talked to me today about the party," Shelley said, watching Jackie. "His father told him about it."

Jackie stopped stirring the chili. "Really?" she said. "What else did he say?"

"He said the party was really loud," Shelley said. "I could have just died."

"Is that all he said?" Jackie questioned.

Is there something else Ted should have said? Shelley wondered. Then she said, "I don't want to talk about Ted. What we ought to talk about is you."

"Are you picking on me?" Jackie cried. She turned to look at Shelley angrily. "Why don't you get off my case?"

"Jackie, what was wrong with you last night?" Shelley asked.

"Nothing's wrong with me—nothing at all,"

Jackie shouted. "Leave me alone, okay?"

Shelley took a deep breath. "You were asleep on the floor when I came home," she told her sister. "And I heard you crying in the middle of the night. That's not normal." Shelley bit her lip. "If you don't want to tell me what's wrong, maybe you should go talk to Dr. Baker. You have to do something. I'm really worried about you."

Jackie laughed. It was a harsh sound. "You're starting to sound like Mom," she said. "You're worrying over nothing. Forget it, and do your homework."

"Jackie, I'm your sister. I just want to help you," Shelley said. "Is that so strange?"

"I can take care of myself," Jackie said. "I told you there's nothing wrong with me. Here, you stir the chili. I have to get ready for class."

Jackie left the kitchen and ran upstairs. Shelley stirred the chili for a while, then decided it was done. She ate a bowl of chili and drank some milk. She sat staring through the window at the backyard. Jackie isn't telling me the truth, Shelley thought. But I don't know how to do anything about it.

Bootsie meowed for a long time before Shelley realized what she was hearing. She jumped up guiltily and fixed his dish. Then she took it outside.

"Well, Bootsie," she said to the cat, "what do I do now?" She sat down on the wall to watch him eat.

Bootsie finished his dinner and licked his whiskers. Then he hopped into Shelley's lap and began to purr. He was a heavy warm weight on her legs.

"Mom and Dad said Jackie and I should take care of each other," Shelley told the cat. "But it's not working that way at all." She buried her face in the cat's soft fur.

Footsteps sounded on the walk as the screen door banged. "I'm leaving for class," Jackie said. Her voice was high and brittle. Shelley saw that her sister's cheeks were flushed, and her eyes were bright. "Don't wait up for me," Jackie added.

"Your class is over at eight thirty," Shelley called after Jackie. "Aren't you coming home then?"

Jackie didn't answer. She threw her shoulder bag into the car and hopped in after it. Shelley watched as the little red car spun out of the driveway.

"Come on, Bootsie," Shelley said. "You can sleep with me again tonight." She dropped her head and carried Bootsie inside. The house had never felt so empty.

* * * * *

Shelley woke in the night when she heard Jackie's car pull into the driveway. She looked at her clock. It was four thirty. She didn't get up. She lay in bed listening to Jackie downstairs in the kitchen. It sounded like she was fixing something to eat. Shelley stared at the ceiling, hugging the cat. She went back to sleep before Jackie came upstairs to bed.

When Shelley got up at seven, she showered and dressed. With Bootsie at her heels, she ran down the stairs and into the kitchen. She gasped. The room was a wreck. There were dirty dishes and pans everywhere. There was food burned on the stove. And the refrigerator door was ajar. Shelley closed it.

"I'm not cleaning up this mess," Shelley said out loud. She pulled a piece of paper out of her notebook. She printed "Jackie, clean this up, now!" in large black letters. Her hand shook as she taped the note to the refrigerator. How dare Jackie go off to work and leave the kitchen like this? she thought.

Shelley made a fast peanut butter and jelly sandwich, wrapped it, and stuffed it into her jacket pocket. "I'll take my breakfast with me," she said. "I can't eat in this mess." Good grief I'm talking to myself, she thought. Well, it's no wonder. Who wouldn't?

Shelley grabbed her books and started outside. Jackie's car was parked in the driveway, so she hadn't left for work after all. Shelley started to go back into the house to check on Jackie. Then she stopped. Jackie told me she could take care of herself, Shelley thought.

Shelley bit at her thumbnail. Then she looked at her watch. There wouldn't be time to wake up Jackie before the school bus would arrive. "So take care of yourself, Jackie," Shelley said, still angry about the mess in the kitchen.

The yellow bus pulled up at the corner, and Shelley got on. Ted was sitting halfway back on the aisle. He leaned out as Shelley approached. "Hey, Jackie's still home," he said. "I thought she worked."

"So?" Shelley snapped. "It's none of your concern," she tossed back as she rushed past him.

Shelley took a seat, biting her lip. I wish I hadn't said that, she thought. I'll bet Ted thinks I have a rotten temper.

Shelley couldn't eat her peanut butter sandwich. She was sure she'd spoiled her chances with Ted. She was too embarrassed even to look at him. It's all because of Jackie,

Shelley thought. If Jackie weren't my sister, I'd hate her.

When the bus reached the school, Shelley waited to get off the bus until everyone else had left. She didn't want to bump into Ted. By the time she got off the bus, she was angry at the world. Nothing's going right. And it's all Jackie's fault, Shelley thought.

Eight

BY Thursday, Shelley wasn't sure if she could last until her parents got home. Jackie had become impossible to live with. She avoided Shelley in the house, and she was gone a lot. When Jackie was home, though, she was either moody or far too happy and talkative. It was as if Jackie were two different people. Shelley never knew which one to expect next.

What worried Shelley more was that Jackie didn't seem to care if her hair was shampooed or not. And she'd worn the same top—with a mustard stain on it—for three days. When Shelley had mentioned it, Jackie blew up. In fact, almost anything Shelley said seemed to make Jackie angry.

Shelley felt completely out of place at home. Jackie was keeping the upstairs phone in her room. She was in there most of the time—

when she was at home at all—and Jo Ellen was with her. It was as if Shelley didn't belong there at all. She had tried to talk to Jackie about it, but Jackie blew up again. So Shelley said very little to Jackie, and she didn't talk to Jo Ellen at all.

It had become a relief to leave the house for school, even though Shelley felt uncomfortable around Ted. He kept trying to talk to her in the hall between classes, but she'd managed to avoid him. She was glad she had Cindy. Cindy never changed. She was always the same cheerful Cindy. And Shelley needed that.

Shelley found herself being grateful for cheerleading practice each afternoon. It kept her away from home for that much longer. And she got to be with Cindy that much more.

* * * * *

After practice on Thursday, Cindy and Shelley changed back into their jeans. Cindy chattered away to Shelley. "Why don't I spend the night with you Friday?" she suggested. "Maybe we can see Ted. We haven't been working on our master plan lately. Have you noticed that Ashley's not talking to Ted? Isn't that wild?"

"Why don't I spend the night with you

instead?" Shelley asked quickly. The thought of Cindy at home with Jackie and Jo Ellen made her sick. "I haven't been to your house for ages."

"Well, Ted doesn't live across the street from me," Cindy pointed out.

Shelley shrugged. "That's okay."

"Hey, what's happened?" Cindy asked, staring at Shelley. "Is there something you haven't told me?"

"I just lost interest in Ted, I guess," Shelley said. She felt guilty as soon as she said it. I don't want to talk about Ted, but I don't have to lie to my best friend, she thought. "Cindy," Shelley said in a rush, "I really do want to spend the night with you tomorrow. Please?"

"You're mad at Ted about something," Cindy guessed. "Look, we don't have to talk about it if you don't want to. Sure, come on over tomorrow after school. I understand. You just don't want to see Ted right now."

"That's not it, exactly," Shelley said. "You are my best friend, you know. I want to spend some time with you."

"Oh," Cindy said, looking pleased. "Well, do you want to do anything special—go to a movie or something like that?"

"I don't think so," Shelley said. "I just want to talk. You know, the usual."

"Well," Cindy said, giggling. "We'll have to gag Jimmy. You know how he is."

Shelley laughed. Suddenly she felt better. Mom and Dad won't be gone that much longer, she thought. When they come home, things will get back to normal. They'll do something about Jackie. And I have Friday night to look forward to.

The girls packed their outfits into their bags and left the gym. Cindy's mother was waiting for her in the car when they got outside.

"Jackie's been picking you up late this week, hasn't she?" Cindy remarked. "She's never here when Mom is."

"Yes, she's been late," Shelley said, crossing her fingers. "Do you think you ought to clear my visit with your mother? I'll wait while you ask her."

Cindy giggled. "Don't you remember? She thinks you're a good influence on me. You can come over any time."

Shelley laughed. When Cindy left, Shelley walked to the city bus stop. She noticed the weather was beautiful. The sky was a brilliant blue, and the air was almost as warm as spring. Shelley grinned as she got on the bus. She was thinking about Cindy's remark that her mother thought Shelley was a good influence.

But as the bus slowed to a stop two blocks from Shelley's home, she began to feel down again. I'm certainly not a good influence on Jackie, she thought, getting off the bus. I can't even get her to talk to me.

Shelley walked to her house and up the path to the kitchen door. She opened the door and went in. Jo Ellen and Jackie were sitting at the table. There was a huge bowl of popcorn between them, and there was more popcorn scattered on the floor.

"Well, if it isn't little Shelley," Jo Ellen drawled.

"Don't you ever go home?" Shelley demanded. "Don't you have a job to go to or something?"

"Hey, she just talked to me," Jo Ellen exclaimed. "Look, Jackie, the kid talked to me. How about that?"

I'm not talking to you, I'm talking at you. There's a difference, Shelley thought. "What's all this popcorn on the floor?" she asked.

"Watch." Jackie giggled. She flipped a kernel of popcorn into the air and tried to catch it in her mouth. When it bounced away, she laughed wildly. So did Jo Ellen. Then Jackie started to do it again.

Shelley snatched the kernel from Jackie's hand. "Stop that," she cried. "What's wrong with you? Why are you doing that?"

"We're just having a little fun," Jo Ellen said, laughing. She started throwing popcorn at Shelley. Jackie laughed even harder. Tears ran down her cheeks, but she couldn't seem to stop laughing.

"Oh, help," Jackie gasped weakly, and began to throw popcorn at Jo Ellen, handful after handful.

Shelley stared at her sister. She took a step back, and then another. Then she whirled around and ran from the house to the garage. Her eyes burned with tears. She pulled open the side door and sank down on a wooden box just inside.

Shelley's chest hurt. She wrapped her arms across it and rocked back and forth on the box. She'd made it through the week by telling herself her parents would be home soon. But things just kept getting worse.

Bootsie put a paw on Shelley's knee and meowed. He'd followed her into the garage.

"I can't stand it, Bootsie," Shelley said. "I don't know if I can last until Monday." She gathered up the cat and held him close, still rocking. "I won't go back in the house," Shelley told Bootsie. "I'll sit out here all night if I have to."

Shelley thought about calling Mrs. White to

see if she could stay there. But she knew she couldn't do that. There would be too many questions. "I'm stuck," she told the cat drearily.

Shelley stayed in the garage for what seemed like hours. Bootsie began to meow for his supper, but she ignored him. Shelley knew he was hungry, but she didn't want to go into the house to fix his food. Who knows what's going on in there? she thought.

It was almost dark when Shelley heard voices. She stood up and looked out the door. Jackie and Jo Ellen were putting things into Jackie's car. Shelley saw Jackie put a lamp into the trunk. It was the lamp from Jackie's room. While Shelley wondered why, Jackie and Jo Ellen went back into the house. They came out carrying Jackie's stereo between them. They put it into the trunk, too.

Shelley rushed out of the garage, nearly tripping over the cat. "What are you doing?" she called. "Jackie?"

There was no answer. Jackie backed out of the driveway fast. The car sped down the street, leaving Shelley on the lawn staring at it.

"Shelley?" a voice called.

Shelley spun around. Ted was coming across the yard toward her. "Hi," he said, looking uncomfortable.

"Well, hi," Shelley said. She wondered how much Ted had seen.

"Could I talk to you for a minute, Shelley?" Ted asked

"What about?" Shelley replied, startled by the question.

Ted moved closer to Shelley. "What's happening at your house?" he asked in a low voice. "What's happening with your sister?" he went on.

"I don't know what you mean," Shelley said blankly.

"Shelley, you know Ginny and Jackie used to be good friends," Ted said. "They used to party together. Ginny and I were talking, and she told me about Jackie's problem."

"What problem?" Shelley cried, beginning to feel angry.

"Look, it's okay," Ted said. "Nobody's running Jackie down. I'm just trying to tell you that my sister said . . ."

"Ginny has no right to be talking about Jackie," Shelley said.

"Hey, wait," Ted told Shelley. "Ginny just wants to help. And I thought maybe I should be the one to talk to you instead of Ginny."

"I don't need your help," Shelley said. "You can tell your sister we're just fine, okay?"

Ted shrugged. "Suit yourself. But we're

here if you want to talk."

Shelley wished the ground would open up
and swallow her. She couldn't stand to look at
Ted for another minute. "There's nothing to
talk about," she said. She turned and walked
into the house as fast as she could.

"I won't think about it," Shelley told
Bootsie as she fixed his supper. She wondered
if all the neighbors were talking about Jackie.
If only Jackie hadn't had that stupid party
Saturday night. That's when all the trouble
started, Shelley thought.

Shelley cleaned up the kitchen, trying to
keep busy so she wouldn't have time to think.
Then she went upstairs to pack her overnight
bag. If she took it to school with her, she could
go straight to Cindy's after school without
coming home first.

While she was packing, a hopeful idea came
to her. If Jackie came back all weird again
tonight, maybe Cindy's mother could come
pick Shelley up. After all, she was already
packed. But as soon as she thought of it, she
knew she couldn't do it. She couldn't get
Cindy's mother involved. What could I say to
her? Shelley thought unhappily. No, I'm stuck.
I'll have to wait for Mom and Dad.

Shelley wandered downstairs and turned on
the television. She sat in front of it, not even

knowing what she was watching. Finally, she turned off the television and locked the house for the night.

Nine

UPSET and angry, Shelley went off to school Friday morning. There was no sign that Jackie had been home at all. Shelley wanted to stay home in case Jackie showed up. She wanted to ask why Jackie had taken those things from the house last night. But she couldn't. There was an important English test coming up first period that Shelley couldn't afford to skip.

Jackie won't spoil my plans for tonight, though, Shelley thought. I'm going to Cindy's. Shelley's mind was made up. But she was still worried about Jackie. She planned to call Jackie's work when she got to school—just to be sure Jackie was there.

When Shelley got to school, she shoved her overnight bag in her locker and pulled out her books. Then she hurried to the pay phone.

Shelley opened the telephone book and ran

her finger down the list of industries in the yellow pages. Finally she found the number she needed. She punched the number in quickly before she could change her mind.

"Web Industries," a voice said. "May I help you?"

"May I speak to Jackie Carter?" Shelley asked.

"Please hold," the voice replied smoothly. Shelley looked down the hall and saw that it was empty. The buzzer had sounded for classes to begin before the voice came back on the phone.

"Who's calling, please?" the voice asked.

"This is her sister," Shelley said. "May I speak with Jackie, please?"

There was a pause. "You could try to reach her at home," the voice said then.

"Didn't she come to work this morning?" Shelley persisted. "I have to know."

"Yes, but. . .she left about half an hour ago."

"Oh. Thanks," Shelley said. So Jackie went to work without coming home to get ready, Shelley thought. She must have stayed all night at Jo Ellen's.

Shelley suddenly remembered her English test. She rushed down the hall. Jackie's probably sick, Shelly thought, beginning to worry again. She wouldn't have left work if she felt okay.

Shelley slipped into English class and took a seat at the back. I'll call Jackie after school and make sure she's all right, Shelley decided. Then she settled down to the test questions the teacher handed her.

* * * * *

"Hurry up, Shelley," Cindy urged. "Mom's out there waiting for us." She danced from one foot to the other impatiently.

"Just a minute, okay?" Shelley stood in the booth with the phone to her ear. School was over, and she wanted to hear Jackie's voice before she went to Cindy's. She almost shut the door to the booth while she waited, but she knew she couldn't. Cindy would wonder about it.

The phone rang and rang. Finally Shelley heard Jackie's voice. "Hello?" Shelley let out her breath in relief. Jackie was home.

"This is me," Shelley announced. "Did you see my note?"

"Oh, sure. You and Cindy have a good time. I'm going to watch television and turn in early," Jackie said. "I'm beat."

"You're not sick or anything, are you?"

Shelley asked anxiously.

Jackie laughed. "Good grief," she said. "Quit worrying about me, will you? I'm just tired, hon. Have fun at Cindy's."

"Okay, then," Shelley said, and then hung up.

Shelley and Cindy hurried out to the waiting car. "What was that all about?" Cindy asked, looking puzzled. "You didn't tell me Jackie had been sick."

"She hasn't," Shelley said defensively. "She's okay. There isn't anything wrong with Jackie."

Cindy gave Shelley an odd look as they climbed into the car, but she didn't pursue it. Instead, she chattered about school and hamburgers and boys and clothes all the way to her house. And after a great fried chicken dinner, Cindy and Shelley talked and giggled some more.

Jimmy finally groaned his way to bed at his mother's orders. That left Cindy and Shelley free to try on makeup and paint their nails three colors. By the time they yawned up the stairs, Shelley had forgotten all about Jackie. She'd almost forgotten how it felt to just be herself. It felt good.

Shelley fell asleep as soon as her head touched the pillow. She woke the next morning full of energy. "What are we going to do today?" she asked, flinging her pillow at Cindy in the other twin bed.

Cindy rolled over and opened one eye. "Do you want to go fishing?" she asked in a blurry voice. "Dad's going."

"Fishing? You mean, with worms and hooks? Oh, yuck," Shelley said with her eyebrows up.

"It'll be fun. Come on, let's have breakfast," Cindy insisted, climbing out of bed.

* * * * *

After a big breakfast, the girls and Jimmy joined Mr. Brooks in the car. They drove to the river and unpacked the fishing gear. The sun was golden, and the green river moved slowly past their feet as Shelley and Cindy talked. Cindy's father had taken Jimmy upstream, leaving the two girls on the bank.

Shelley looked up at the gloriously blue sky. She sighed, thinking how peaceful it was. . . and how peaceful it wasn't at home any more. Not with Jackie there. . . .

"Is something on your mind?" Cindy asked idly.

"It's just that I don't want to go home," Shelley found herself saying. Her eyes filled with tears. She brushed them away with the back of her hand, hoping Cindy hadn't noticed.

"I knew there was something wrong," Cindy said, watching the water. "It's Jackie, isn't it?"

Shelley couldn't speak for a moment. Cindy knows me so well, she thought. Maybe—just maybe—Cindy would understand after all. "Could I. . . Could I stay over tonight, too? I. . .," Shelley had to stop. She couldn't talk past the lump in her throat.

"Jimmy's going to Grandma's for the night," Cindy said, not looking at Shelley. "Is Jackie okay by herself? I mean, I don't know what the problem is yet."

"She'll be all right. Thanks, Cindy," Shelley said. She took a deep breath. "I'll call Jackie when we get back to your house and tell her I'm staying all night with you again. Oh, Cindy." Shelley began to cry.

"Hey, listen," Cindy said. "We'll get it figured out—you and me, okay? Don't worry." She grinned, and Shelley had to smile back, even though she didn't feel much like smiling.

* * * * *

"You should have told me," Cindy said. They'd gone to Cindy's room as soon as they got back from the river. Cindy was sitting on her bed cross-legged, staring at Shelley. Her eyes looked very serious.

Shelley sighed. "I know that now. I. . . Well, I didn't think I could talk to you about it. I didn't want you to think Jackie's an awful person, I guess. Do you think it's those freaky friends of hers? Maybe she's trying to be like them?"

Cindy shook her head. "I don't know," she said. "From what you've said, it's like she's really up and then all the way down. I don't know how you can even stand to stay with her, especially after that crazy party." Cindy shivered. "My gosh, what are your mom and dad going to say?"

"I don't know," Shelley confessed. She felt relieved that she'd told Cindy. But having to talk about everything that happened had upset her. "Cindy, do you think Jackie is mentally ill?" Shelley asked hopelessly. "Maybe that's what Ted was trying to talk to me about."

"Ted? Ted talked to you about Jackie?" Cindy asked, looking startled. "You didn't tell me that."

"Oh. Well, he tried to talk to me Thursday night—by my driveway."

"By your driveway?" Cindy breathed. "You mean, he came over there to talk to you? I can't believe you didn't call me right then."

"It wasn't like that," Shelley said. "He came over and told me Ginny wanted to help me with Jackie. And he said that he and Ginny were there if I wanted to talk. It really made me mad," Shelley added.

"Oh, Shelley," Cindy said. She clapped her hands over her mouth. "Oh, Shelley," she repeated.

"What is it?" Shelley asked. "Why are you looking at me like that?"

"What else did Ted say?" Cindy asked.

"Well, he said something about Jackie's problem. I don't know what he meant, though," Shelley told her.

Cindy shook her head. Then she looked straight at Shelley. "Ted's sister used to be on drugs. My mom told me. I thought you knew."

"What?" Shelley exclaimed. "But she's okay."

"She is now," Cindy said. "She stopped using drugs and started taking care of herself. Shelley, could Jackie be on drugs?"

"No," Shelley cried. "Jackie wouldn't do that." But even as she said it, she had the awful feeling that it might be true. It would explain so much. And Ted had said Ginny and Jackie used to party together. Shelley had forgotten that. "Oh, Cindy," Shelley gasped. "What if it's true?"

Cindy looked worried. "It could be what's the matter with her," she said. "Don't you remember the film we saw at school—the one about drug users? A lot of what you've told me fits that film."

"What will I do?" Shelley asked frantically.

"You'll have to talk to your mom and dad," Cindy insisted. "If that's it, she needs help, like Ted said."

"I can't go to Mom and Dad with this," Shelley wailed. "I just can't. What if it's not true?"

"You'd better think about it," Cindy said. "If it's true, it will just get worse. She might die. And if it's not true, there's still something really wrong with her."

Shelley got up from the other bed where she was sitting. She began to pace back and forth. "I don't know what to do," she said.

"How was Jackie when you called her after we got home from the river?" Cindy asked. "Did she sound okay when you told her you were staying over tonight, too?"

"I didn't talk to her," Shelley said. "Jo Ellen answered the phone." She began to cry.

Cindy jumped to her feet. "Look," she told Shelley. "You can't do anything until your parents get home, right? That's just the day after tomorrow." She found the tissue box and handed it to Shelley.

Shelley took a tissue and blew her nose. "That's right," she said. "I have until Monday to figure out what to say to Mom and Dad. Oh, Cindy, what a mess this is."

Ten

SHELLEY went to church with Cindy's family the next morning. After she'd talked to Cindy, she felt better about things. She still wasn't sure Jackie's problem was drugs, but she knew something was wrong. And she knew she had to talk to her parents about it when they got home.

Outside in the bright morning sunlight, Shelley turned to her friend. "It really helped me to talk to you, Cindy," Shelley said.

"What are friends for?" Cindy asked. "Are you sure you want us to drop you off at your house?" Cindy looked around for her parents. "You can always go home with us, you know."

"No, I'd better go home," Shelley said. "Jackie might need me, you know? But thanks, Cindy."

"Look, there's Mom," Cindy said. "And here comes Dad with Jimmy and Grandma."

"You really have a nice family," Shelley said wistfully, watching them approach.

"So do you, Shelley," Cindy told her. "Try not to worry, okay?"

Shelley promised, but she did begin to worry again on the way home. Which Jackie would she find when she got there, she wondered, the sister she'd grown up with or the stranger who cried in the night?

As the Brooks' car turned the corner into Shelley's street, Cindy sat straight up in the backseat. "Isn't that your dad's car, Shelley?" she asked, pointing.

Cindy was right. There was her dad's car, sitting in the driveway.

Shelley could hardly believe it. "They're home," she said, excited. "Cindy, they're home."

"They're a day early, too, aren't they?" Mr. Brooks remarked. "I'll bet you'll be glad to see them." He pulled over to the curb and stopped in front of the house.

Shelley bounced out of the car. "I can't wait to see Mom and Dad," she exclaimed.

"Just a minute," Cindy called. "Don't forget your bag." She jumped out of the car and handed the bag to Shelley. "Call me later," she said quickly.

"I will," Shelley promised. "Thank you for

having me over, Mrs. Brooks. . .Mr. Brooks,"
she added, and ran for the house.

"Mom? Dad? I'm home," Shelley shouted as
she burst into the living room.

"Oh, honey," Shelley's mother said, rushing
in from the hall. "I missed you so much. John,
the girls are home," she called back over her
shoulder. She grabbed Shelley in a big hug as
Shelley's father came into the living room
behind her.

"I missed you, too," he said. "Give me a
hug, honey. Say, we timed this just right. We
wanted to be here when you got home from
church. Surprised?"

"I sure am," Shelley said. She laughed. "I
love you, Dad. I'm so glad you and Mom are
home. Why are you a day early?"

"The meetings went better than we thought
they would," her dad said. "It cut a day off the
trip. I even had time to do some shopping with
your mother. I wish you could have come
along, though. You would have really enjoyed
it. So would Jackie."

"You won't believe this," Shelley's mother
told her. "We actually got to attend a real
masquerade party. There was a big orchestra,
a six-course dinner—the works."

"You mean, with costumes and those little
black masks and everything?" Shelley asked,

impressed. "How did you work that?"

"One of Dad's business friends wangled an invitation for us," Shelley's mother explained, giving Shelley another hug. "But all I could think about while we were there was how much my girls would have enjoyed it."

"Did you buy out Paris?" Shelley asked.

Shelley's father rolled his eyes. "It's being shipped after us," he said. "Your mother went wild in the shops."

"Now, John," Shelley's mother said. "I didn't spend all my time shopping. There were the museums and the art galleries, and..."

"She had a good time," Shelley's father said, grinning.

"I had a wonderful time. But it's good to be home," Shelley's mother added. "I missed my girls."

"Why isn't Jackie coming in?" Shelley's father asked, starting toward the door.

Shelley froze. "She's not here?" she asked.

"What do you mean?" her mother asked, looking surprised. "Didn't she go to church with you?"

"No. No, she didn't," Shelley said.

Shelley's father turned around to stare at Shelley. "Well, how did you get home from church?"

"I went to church with Cindy. Her dad

brought me home," Shelley said. "Isn't Jackie's car in the garage?"

Shelley's father left the room. "I spent the night with Cindy, Mom," Shelly explained. "I thought Jackie was here."

"Maybe she left a note," Shelley's mother said.

Shelley's father came back into the room. "You're right, Shelley. Her car's in the garage. Where is she?"

"She must have slept in," Shelley said quickly. Her throat was dry. "I'll run up and look, okay?"

Shelley rushed up the stairs. Oh, Jackie, she thought, please be there. Please be asleep in your room. Shelley grabbed the doorknob to Jackie's room, but the door was locked.

Shelley knocked on the door. "Jackie, unlock the door. Mom and Dad are home." There was no answer. She knocked again, harder.

"Is Jackie up there?" Shelley's mother called from downstairs.

Shelley ran back to the top of the stairs, upset. "Her door's locked. I can't get in," she shouted.

"What is this?" Shelley's father said. "What do you mean, the door's locked? We don't lock bedroom doors here," he went on, coming

101

quickly up the stairs. Shelley's mother was right behind him. He started for Jackie's room. "Jackie? Are you in there?" he said loudly. He knocked on the door.

"She'd be awake by now if she were in there," Shelley's mother said. "She must have spent the night with a friend. But why would she lock her bedroom door?"

"Mom, I just know she's in there," Shelley said. She was shaking so she could hardly get the words out.

Shelley's mother stared at her. "Shelley, what's wrong here?" she asked. "Why are you so upset?"

"Jackie's been locking her door ever since you left for Paris—whether she's in her room or not," Shelley said. "But I just know she's in there now."

"Why would she do that?" her mother asked. "Shelley, what's going on?"

"I don't know. I don't know," Shelley repeated. "There's something wrong with her. I don't know what it is," she said, wringing her hands.

"Jackie, open the door," her father shouted, pounding on the door. "Are you all right?"

"John, we have to get in there," Shelley's mother said. "Something's wrong with Jackie."

Shelley's father stepped back and lunged at

the door with his shoulder. He twisted the knob as his shoulder hit the door and Shelley heard a sharp crackling sound. Then he forced the door open. He rushed into the room and Shelley heard him make an awful sound.

Shelley pushed in past her mother. Jackie was lying crumpled up on her side in the bed. She was still and white. "Mom...Dad. Is she all right?" Shelley gasped.

Shelley's mother reached for Jackie's hand. "She's so cold—and I can't find a pulse. Oh, John," she cried, looking up at her husband.

"I should never have gone to Cindy's. I should never have left her," Shelley said, terrified. "Will...Will she die? She won't die, will she, Mom?"

"We'll have to call the emergency squad," Shelley's father said. He grabbed the phone from Jackie's bedside table and started punching in the emergency number.

"What's wrong with her? Do you have any idea, Shelley?" her mother asked. "Has she been sick?"

"We have an emergency here," Shelley's father said rapidly into the phone. "Forty-four Westerbridge Road. It's our daughter."

"Shelley?" her mother repeated. "Do you know what's wrong with Jackie?" Her eyes were frantic as she looked at Shelley.

The floor seemed to tilt beneath Shelley's feet. "I. . ." she began, and then started over. "I think she's on drugs," she blurted out. "I didn't know what to do," she cried, and burst into tears.

Shelley's father stared at her from across the bed. "Dear God. It might be an overdose," he said into the phone. "Yes, hurry."

*　*　*　*　*

Shelley sat on the wall by the kitchen door, clutching the cat. Bootsie was complaining at being held too tightly, but Shelley didn't even hear his cries. The emergency squad had arrived in minutes. They'd cleared the room as soon as they saw Jackie. They were still upstairs working with her.

Mom and Dad were in the house, but Shelley had rushed outside, away from the sounds from upstairs. She stared at the flashing lights on the emergency vehicle parked in the street and tried not to think. She'd never felt so alone.

"Shelley," Ted said. "Shelley, can I help?"

Shelley hadn't heard Ted coming. She looked up, startled. Bootsie escaped, jumping away and Ted sat down on the wall with Shelley.

"It's Jackie, isn't it?" Ted asked. "I just knew it had to be Jackie."

"Oh, Ted," Shelley said. "Jackie's so sick." She started to cry again. "I told Mom and Dad. I told them she might be on drugs. Ted, do you really think she is?"

"I know where you're coming from," Ted told her. "I've been there. Ginny was a user."

Shelley nodded. "Cindy told me. I'm sorry, Ted."

"It was bad," Ted admitted. "Believe me, I know how you feel." He took Shelley's hand and held it.

"But are you sure about Jackie?" Shelley asked, still hoping it wasn't true. "How can you be sure?"

Ted looked away. "Ginny and Jackie—well, you know how close they were. They were good friends. Ginny's talked to me about it, Shelley. They fell in with a crowd that used drugs, and before long they were trying it, too. Then when Ginny pulled out of the scene, she tried to get Jackie to stop. And that's when they stopped being friends."

Shelley couldn't think of anything to say. Ted turned to face her. "Don't kid yourself," he told Shelley. "I tried to do that, too. I didn't want to believe my sister had a problem. It doesn't work that way. That's why I tried to talk to you about Jackie."

"I couldn't understand why you were saying those things to me," Shelley said.

"I thought you'd make the connection. I hoped you'd talk to your folks and get help for Jackie," Ted said. "I hope she's all right. They haven't told you anything yet, have they?"

There was a flurry of activity inside the house. Shelley jumped to her feet. "Mom?" she cried. "What's happening?"

Shelley's mother and father ran out the kitchen door. "They're taking Jackie out the front way. We're to follow them to the hospital," Shelley's father said. He ran toward the car.

"Shelley, are you coming?" her mother asked, following her husband.

"Go on, Shelley," Ted said. "They need you."

Shelley rushed after her parents and slid into the backseat. "Will Jackie be all right?" she asked. "What did they say?"

Shelley's father backed out of the driveway fast and stopped the car behind the emergency vehicle. The squad was just lifting Jackie's stretcher into the back. Then they slammed the doors shut and drove off.

"They do think it's drugs," Shelley's mother told her. Her face was as white as Jackie's had been. "They think they got her in time."

The car lurched as Shelley's father threw it into gear. Shelley watched the flashing red lights ahead as they followed Jackie to the hospital. She was afraid to think about what might happen.

Eleven

SHELLEY stared across the crowded
waiting room outside the intensive care
unit of the third floor of the hospital. She'd
been there all day with her mom and dad, and
it had been the longest day of her life.

Shelley had called Cindy when they got
there. She called her again when Dr. Baker
came in to tell them Jackie wasn't out of
danger yet. Then Shelley told her mom and
dad everything that had happened at home
while they were gone. She didn't want to talk
about it, but they had to know. When that was
over, there was nothing for Shelley to do but
to wait.

Shelley noticed that the child who'd been
running all over the room earlier was asleep on
his mother's lap. She watched the woman
smooth the little boy's hair as he slept.
Somehow it made her want to cry.

She shifted restlessly in her chair. "How much longer do you think it will be before we know about Jackie?" Shelley asked her mother for the tenth time.

Her mother sighed and put down the magazine she'd been leafing through. "Nobody knows, Shelley," she replied. "You heard Dr. Baker. She was in serious condition when they got her here."

Shelley's father had been sitting with his head in his hands. Now he lifted his head and looked into space. "I still don't understand how this could have happened," he muttered. "Jackie was all right when we left for Europe. And then to come home and find her like this. I still can't believe it."

Shelley's mother turned to her husband. "I know. I felt like that, too, at first. But, John, I've had a lot of time to think today," she said. "Jackie's changed. She's changed so much that I can't believe I didn't see it. I kept telling myself she was having a hard time growing up—learning to be on her own, instead of dependent on us."

"Yes," Shelley's father said slowly. "You're right, Karen. Jackie's a different girl now. Remember when we counted on her being there for Shelley's birthday? We didn't even know where she was for two days."

"We were worried sick," Shelley's mother said. "It just wasn't like Jackie. She'd always been so reliable."

"She doesn't see her old friends any more," Shelley said. "I found that out when she came to stay with me. None of them called. And I didn't know anybody at that party."

"She didn't want us to meet any of her new friends," Shelley's dad added. "That should have told us something. She always had her old gang of friends at the house. Remember, Karen?"

"I asked her what happened to some of her old friends, John," Shelley's mother said. "Jackie simply blew up at me. I'd never seen her like that. And she was suspicious of things I'd say to her—she kept accusing me of picking on her."

"She did that to me, too, Mom," Shelley put in. "I couldn't talk to her about anything that mattered. It just made her mad."

"I've been thinking about this new job of Jackie's," Shelley's mother said. "I think she was fired from her last job. I don't think she quit it for a better one. There are too many things that don't add up."

"Everything Shelley's told us about the last two weeks just shows me how blind I've been," Shelley's father said. "Why didn't we realize what was going on sooner, before this happened? She's our daughter. Why didn't we know?" He pulled out his handkerchief and wiped his eyes.

Shelley's mother put her arm around her husband. "John, we just couldn't believe it could happen to our Jackie. I thought it only happened to other people's children."

"Like Ginny Hayes," Shelley added. "Mom, did you know about Ginny?"

"Yes, Shelley, I did. But I didn't know you knew," her mother said, looking at her. "I see now we should have talked about Ginny. I'm ashamed to tell you this, but at the time I was just glad it wasn't Jackie. I guess it did cross my mind after all that Jackie might be using drugs. I didn't want to believe it, so I put it out of my mind."

"We have no choice but to believe it now," Shelley's dad said. He groaned. "Jackie's in intensive care, and she may even..."

"Don't say it," Shelley's mother said quickly. "We have to believe Jackie's going to be all right." She bit her lip.

Shelley stood up suddenly. She tried to smile at her mother. "I'm going to take a walk," she said. If I don't get away for a while I'm going to be sick, she thought.

Shelley headed blindly across the waiting

room and into the hall. She leaned against the wall with her eyes shut. What will I do if Jackie does die? she thought hopelessly. I can't stand this. I can't lose my sister.

Shelley felt a hand on her arm and opened her eyes. Ginny Hayes stood there. She looked at Shelley for a long moment and then hugged her. "How is Jackie?" Ginny asked. "Is she going to be all right?"

"I don't know. They haven't told us yet," Shelley said. She started to cry, and searched her pocket for a tissue.

"I'm so sorry, Shelley," Ginny said. "When Ted told me about this, I couldn't stay home. I thought I might be able to help—maybe sit with your folks until you know how Jackie is."

"Oh, thanks, Ginny," Shelley said. "Mom and Dad will appreciate it. You and Jackie were so close all those years. . ." Shelley's throat was so tight she had to stop talking.

"I've never stopped caring about Jackie," Ginny said. "I just wish I'd done more to help. I should have told your mom and dad about Jackie—maybe this wouldn't have happened."

"It's not your fault," Shelley said.

"Do you want me to stay with you?" Ginny asked.

Shelley shook her head. "No. I'll be all right. I don't want to go back in there right now, though. I don't want Mom and Dad to see me like this."

"I'll go on in the waiting room, then," Ginny said. "You take your time." She gave Shelley another hug and left.

Shelley blew her nose. "Hi, Shelley," a voice said from behind her. She turned around to see Ted.

"Oh, Ted," Shelley said. "I'm glad you're here. We don't know anything about Jackie yet."

"I heard. I've been holding up the wall over there," Ted said, nodding across the hall. "Come on, I'll buy you a cola."

"I shouldn't leave," Shelley said uncertainly.

"There's a snack bar on this floor," Ted told her. "You've been here all day. You need a break. They'll page you if they need you. Come on," he said again. He put his arm around Shelley's shoulders and walked her down the hall.

The snack bar was empty. Shelley sank into a chair while Ted got a couple of soft drinks from the machine. He brought them to the little table in the corner and sat down across from Shelley.

"I don't know what to say," Shelley said.

"You don't have to talk," Ted told her. "It's okay." He popped the cans opened and handed one to Shelley.

"I just feel. . .empty," Shelley said. "It's funny. I've been so upset all day, and now it's like I don't feel anything. I'm just. . .waiting, I guess."

"I'll wait with you," Ted said. "That's all right, isn't it? I'll leave if you want me to."

"Don't go," Shelley said quickly. She reached across the table and Ted took her hand. "I told you I was glad you're here, Ted. I meant it. After all, you've been through this with Ginny."

"Ginny never wound up in intensive care," Ted said. He looked at Shelley's hand as he spoke. "I guess she was luckier than Jackie."

"I can't believe this is real," Shelley said. "I know what's happening, but it's almost like a bad dream, you know? It's just so hard to believe that it's happening to my sister."

"I felt like that, too," Ted said. "When I found out Ginny was using drugs, it explained a lot of things, though. I thought she didn't care about me—about Mom and Dad." He shook his head. "I was wrong. It wasn't that at all."

"I guess I've been pretty stupid," Shelley admitted. "I was so looking forward to spending time with Jackie. These last two weeks have been just awful. At least, I know

now that it was because of the drugs. I thought Jackie just didn't have any time for me any more."

"I remember one thing that happened to me," Ted said. "I'd saved up for tickets to that big rock concert last year. I was going to take Ginny." He shrugged. "It was her favorite group. I knew things weren't going well for her. But I didn't know what was wrong. I thought the concert might make her feel better."

"What happened?" Shelley asked.

"When it was time to leave for the concert, she was out of it," Ted said. He looked away. "I tore up the tickets."

"Oh, Ted," Shelley said, sighing. "I'm sorry."

"Yeah. It was bad," Ted said. "I was so mad I could have killed her. I couldn't figure out why she was doing those things to me—to herself."

"How could you know?" Shelley asked. "I didn't know what was wrong with Jackie, either."

"Maybe I should have guessed," Ted said. "I was so sure Ginny was just acting weird—that she didn't want me around any more. I was so angry with her for treating me like that."

Shelley looked down to see that she had

torn her napkin into little squares. "Ted, why did Ginny start using drugs?" she asked. "Do you know? She always seemed so happy."

"I don't know," Ted said. "I think it was for a lot of reasons. It doesn't really matter, does it? What matters is that I have my sister back. It wasn't easy. Mom and Dad and I all worked at it with Ginny."

Shelley pushed the torn napkin aside. She stood up and walked to the window. She looked down at the red and yellow leaves on the old trees that grew on the hospital grounds. But she didn't even see them.

I've acted the same way Ted did, she thought. I haven't been thinking about Jackie at all. I wanted my sister all to myself. And when things went wrong at home, I got mad at Jackie. I didn't stop to think about Jackie—just about me.

"Shelley, are you all right?" Ted asked. He had followed her to the window. "I didn't mean to upset you."

Shelley turned to Ted. Her eyes brimming with tears. "Oh, Ted," she said. "I didn't know. I was so angry with Jackie. Now it may be too late..."

Ted gathered Shelley into his arms. "Don't say that," he said. "Jackie is going to make it." He laid his cheek against her hair and held her without speaking.

Shelley stood quietly for a moment with her face against Ted's jacket. Then she lifted her head and looked up into Ted's face. His eyes were honest and concerned. She suddenly realized that Ted really did care about her. I kept trying to get him to notice me, she thought. And then it just happened, all by itself.

"I've been trying to talk to you, you know," Ted said. It was almost as if he'd read her mind. "I tried at school, and in your yard..."

"I know," Shelley said. "I'm sorry. I've been avoiding you. I've been so wrapped up in my own worries, and I was embarrassed about the party..."

The loudspeaker crackled. Then Shelley heard her name being paged. "Shelley Carter, come to Intensive Care. Shelley Carter, come to Intensive Care."

Shelley froze. Ted took her arm and started for the door. "I'll go with you," he said. "Come on, Shelley. Hurry."

Twelve

THE hall seemed a hundred miles long. By the time Shelley reached the waiting room, she was running. Ted was right behind her. She saw Dr. Baker, wearing greens, across the room with her parents and Ginny.

"Jackie's condition has stabilized," Dr. Baker called as Shelley and Ted neared. "I was starting to tell your parents that I was delayed in emergency surgery, Shelley. That's why it took so long for me to get here to tell you. I'm sorry. I know how worried you've all been."

"Jackie's going to be all right," Shelley's mother said. She was laughing and crying at the same time. "Thank God. Shelley, she's going to be all right."

"That's wonderful news," Shelley's father added, blowing his nose.

"I'm so glad," Ginny exclaimed.

Shelley burst into tears of relief and reached

for her dad's hand. "Are you sure, Dr. Baker?" she managed to ask.

"Jackie's a lucky girl," Dr. Baker said. He shook his head, and pulled off his surgical cap. "It could easily have gone the other way for her. I checked on Jackie just now and talked to the unit supervisor," he went on. "Jackie's waking up. You can go see her now, John."

"May I go, too?" Shelley asked quickly.

"Sure. You can all three go in. Just stay about ten minutes, though," Dr. Baker added. Then he turned to Shelley's father. "Jackie will need to be here for a while. We'll set up a time to discuss her treatment plan." He shook hands with Shelley's dad. "It's a good thing you got Jackie here when you did," he said. "Another hour or two and it would have been too late."

"Ted and I will wait until you've seen Jackie, so we can hear how she's feeling," Ginny said to Shelley's mother. "I'm so glad Jackie came through this."

Mrs. Carter hugged Ginny. "I'm really glad you came, Ginny," she said.

Ted gave Shelley and encouraging smile. "Go give your sister a hug," he said.

* * * * *

Shelley wasn't prepared for what she found

when she entered Jackie's room. The room was dim, with curtains pulled almost shut. Half of the room seemed to be filled with blinking lights. The lights came from several monitors that banked the hospital bed. A constant stream of sound came from them—a steady clicking, with a beeping tone now and then. Jagged lines of green light danced across a screen. And the wires that came down from the monitors all led to the sheeted figure in the bed below.

Shelley's mom and dad had gone around the foot of the bed to the far side. Shelley saw an IV dangling from its stand. Colorless fluid dripped slowly through a clear plastic tube into Jackie's arm. Shelley ducked under the tube to get to Jackie's bedside.

Shelley stared at Jackie. Her eyes were closed. She was so pale that the shadows under her eyes looked like bruises. She looked so small beneath the white sheet drawn up to her chest. It's like she's just barely there, Shelley thought, and shivered. She could hear the hiss of oxygen through the green plastic tubes that went into Jackie's nostrils.

Jackie opened her eyes. She looked confused, and then she focused on her mother. "I. . .I'm sorry," she mumbled. Her voice was hoarse. "Forgive me? Mom. . ."

Jackie's mother bent over the side rail of the bed. "Oh, Jackie, don't," she interrupted softly. "Don't try to talk, honey. Just rest. We love you."

"So sorry. . . Sorry I worried you. . ." Jackie said. "Shelley?" Jackie's hand moved on the sheet, toward Shelley. Shelley grabbed her sister's hand and held it tightly.

"Oh, Jackie, I was so scared," Shelley said. "I'm so glad you're going to be okay." She bent down to hug Jackie. "I love you," Shelley said.

Jackie nodded. Then she looked at her father. "Dad?" she said.

Shelley's father reached to hug Jackie, too. "Honey," he said, crying. "Oh, Jackie."

Jackie shut her eyes and took a breath. "I thought. . .I thought I could take care of myself," she said.

"We can talk later," her father said. "You need to rest now, sweetheart."

"Have to tell you. . ." Jackie murmured. "So sorry for putting you through this. . ." Shelley's mother was rubbing Jackie's free arm. Jackie looked up at her and started to cry. "I tried to stop using drugs, Mom. . ., but I couldn't."

"We understand," her mother said. "Shhh. It's all right. You're going to be all right, Jackie."

"I'd think I could. . .stay away from drugs, and then. . .I had to have them. I couldn't stop.

Jo Ellen. . .My friends. . .always had them around."

Shelley patted her sister's hand. Jackie looked at her sadly. "Locked my door. . .I had drugs in my room. I'm sorry, Shelley. . . ."

"It's okay, Jackie," Shelley said quickly. "Don't worry about that right now."

"Mom?" Jackie said. "I have to tell you something. I took some things from the house. . . not very many. I hocked them." She tried to lift her head from the pillow. "I had to have the money. . .I can't get them back now. I lost my job again."

Shelley's mother looked at Shelley. "I didn't know about the job," Shelley said.

"It isn't important now," Shelley's father said. "The only important thing is getting Jackie better."

Jackie looked confused again. "I thought I'd told you. . .about the job. Oh, I don't know. . . Oh, Mom," she said. Tears were running down her face. "I'm afraid. I'm always afraid now, Mom. I don't know what to do."

"We'll help you," Jackie's mother said, reaching for her. "We'll find a way, Jackie." She hugged Jackie, hard.

"I need your help," Jackie sobbed.

"Jackie," her father said. "I don't know very much about this yet. I don't even know how to help you, but we're all going to help. We'll get through this somehow. We'll do it together."

Shelley heard the door open and looked back over her shoulder. A nurse stood in the doorway, outlined in the bright light from the hall. "It's time to go now," the nurse said quietly. "She needs to rest."

Shelley's father took his wife's arm. "Of course," he said. "We'll be back, Jackie," he promised.

"Just rest, honey," Jackie's mother said. She bent down and kissed Jackie. So did her husband.

"Could I stay just a little bit longer?" Shelley asked the nurse. The nurse hesitated. "Please?" Shelley asked. "There's something I have to say to my sister."

"Shelley, she needs to rest," her mother said. "We really should leave."

"I know, Mom. I just want to stay for a minute," Shelley said. "It's important."

"If it's only for a minute, you can stay," the nurse said.

"We'll be outside," Shelley's father said. "We'll wait for you, Shelley."

Shelley nodded, and her mom and dad left the room. The nurse checked the controls on the monitor and adjusted the IV drip before she followed Shelley's parents out of the room.

Shelley turned back to Jackie. "I want to tell you something before I leave," Shelley said. "I'm sorry. If I'd realized you had a problem, maybe you wouldn't be here. I guess I should have known."

Jackie shook her head slightly. "You didn't do anything," she said. "It's all my fault." She turned her face away from Shelley.

"Don't say that," Shelley said. She took Jackie's hand. "Things have been so different between us that. . .Well, I just thought you didn't want me around any more. It made me so angry that I couldn't see that you needed me."

Jackie closed her eyes. "I'm so tired," she whispered. "I don't know if I can make it."

"We're all going to help," Shelley said. "Just keep thinking about that." She leaned over the bed and kissed her sister's cheek. "I'm not supposed to stay very long," she said. "Is there anything I can do before I go?"

Jackie's mouth twisted. "You can get me a new life," she said.

"Oh, Jackie," Shelley said. Tears filled her eyes. "I can't get a new life for you, but I can help you make a new one." She held Jackie close. "I love you. I really do. . ."

Shelley pressed her cheek against her sister's. She couldn't tell if her face was wet with Jackie's tears or her own, but it didn't matter.

The door sighed open. The nurse stood in the doorway again. "It's time to leave now," she said.

Shelley looked at Jackie. "I'll be back," she said. She turned and walked to the door. Then she turned back to look at her sister again.

Jackie had raised up a bit. Tears shone on her face. She gave Shelley a crooked little smile. "I love you," she said. "I love you."

About the Author

MARCIA KRUCHTEN grew up in the deeply wooded hills of southern Indiana, a setting reflected in many of her books. Her parents were schoolteachers, and she began reading before she was old enough for a library card. From there, the next step was to write stories of her own, drawing pictures to go with them. She planned to become an artist who wrote. Instead, she became a writer who paints.

Marcia attended Indiana University, and worked both as a commercial artist and as a medical records technician. She continued to write while her four children grew up. She now devotes her time to writing for adults as well as for younger readers. When not at the typewriter, Marcia can be found exploring woods and fields in search of the wildflowers and rural scenes she enjoys painting.

Marcia and her husband live in a hundred-year-old house in Bedford, Indiana. It was the scene for another of Marcia's books, *The Ghost in the Mirror.*